Thomas Babington Macaulay

The Life of Samuel Johnson

Thomas Babington Macaulay

The Life of Samuel Johnson

ISBN/EAN: 9783337415334

Printed in Europe, USA, Canada, Australia, Japan

Cover: Foto ©Raphael Reischuk / pixelio.de

More available books at **www.hansebooks.com**

ECLECTIC ENGLISH CLASSICS

THE LIFE

OF

SAMUEL JOHNSON

BY

LORD MACAULAY

NEW YORK ∴ CINCINNATI ∴ CHICAGO

AMERICAN BOOK COMPANY

INTRODUCTION.

THOMAS BABINGTON MACAULAY, the most popular essayist of his time, was born at Leicestershire, Eng., in 1800. His father, Zachary Macaulay, a friend and coworker of Wilberforce, was a man of austere character, who was greatly shocked at his son's fondness for worldly literature. Macaulay's mother, however, encouraged his reading, and did much to foster his literary tastes.

" From the time that he was three," says Trevelyan in his standard biography, " Macaulay read incessantly, for the most part lying on the rug before the fire, with his book on the ground and a piece of bread and butter in his hand." He early showed marks of uncommon genius. When he was only seven, he took it into his head to write a " Compendium of Universal History." He could remember almost the exact phraseology of the books he read, and had Scott's " Marmion " almost entirely by heart. His omnivorous reading and extraordinary memory bore ample fruit in the richness of allusion and brilliancy of illustration that marked the literary style of his mature years. He could have written " Sir Charles Grandison " from memory, and in 1849 he could repeat more than half of " Paradise Lost."

In 1818 Macaulay entered Trinity College, Cambridge. Here he won prizes in classics and English ; but he had an invincible distaste for mathematics.

His " Essay on Milton," published in the " Edinburgh Review " in 1825, made him famous; and his subsequent contributions to that magazine, written in all the vigor of his early years, were eagerly and widely read. Among the best of his essays are those on " Clive," " Warren Hastings," " Frederick the Great," " Addison," " Bunyan," and " Comic Dramatists of the Restoration."

Macaulay possessed great versatility, and made a reputation not only as an essayist, but also as a statesman, orator, poet, and historian. Known as a stanch Whig, he entered Parliament in 1830, where his speeches on the Reform Bill placed him among the foremost orators of the day. He had, however, none of the outward graces of the orator. He spoke rapidly, and with but little emphasis. Yet Gladstone, who sat in Parliament with him, says, " Whenever he rose to speak, it was a summons like a trumpet call to fill the benches."

Many high political honors signalized Macaulay's prosperity. As member of the Supreme Council of India (1834–38), he did yeoman service for the cause of education and judicial reform. After his return from India, he became once more a member of Parliament, and held the office of secretary of war in the Melbourne ministry. Throughout his public career, he maintained his reputation as a true, courageous, and upright man. Devoted as he was to literary studies, he never for a moment allowed them to interfere with his official obligations, or, in fact, with any of the practical duties of life.

Macaulay's " colloquial talents," to quote his language concerning Johnson, " were of the highest order." He was a fluent and fascinating talker, but generally assumed the lion's share of conversation.

One of the most winning things about Macaulay was his love of children, with whom he had the utmost sympathy. The following is an extract from his diary, relating to a gorgeous valentine he had sent to his little niece Alice: "Alice was in perfect raptures over her valentine. She begged quite pathetically to be told the truth about it. When we were alone together, she said, 'I am going to be very serious.' Down she fell before me on her knees and lifted up her hands. 'Dear uncle, do tell the truth to your little girl. Did you send the valentine?' I did not choose to tell a real lie to a child even about such a trifle, and so I owned it."

In 1857 Macaulay was raised to the peerage as Baron Macaulay of Rothley, but lived to enjoy the honor a short time only. He died suddenly and peacefully on the 28th of December, 1859.

Macaulay's fame as a poet rests on those specimens of stirring verse, "Ivry" and "Lays of Ancient Rome," which "every schoolboy knows." His prose masterpiece, however, is the "History of England from the Accession of James II.," the first two volumes of which appeared in 1848. It was a labor of love, written in his more comfortable years, after the competency derived from his Indian office had made possible for him a purely literary life. It is original in treatment, and has all the charm of a fascinating novel.

Macaulay's "style" was unquestionably "the man." He had strong likes and dislikes, and positive convictions. Like Dr. Johnson, he never halted at halfway judgments, nor wore his opinions "on both sides, like a leather jerkin." Naturally, therefore, his language, impetuous and sanguine, is instinct with force and energy. Of a practical turn of mind, he saw clearly, and wrote clearly. Among the features of his celebrated style are the frequent use of antithesis and epigram to make one idea set off another, his fondness for the short sentence, his overflowing historical and literary allusions, his mastery of paragraph structure, and his rapid and picturesque grouping of details. His pictorial method popularized literary criticism, and kindled a great and permanent interest in English history and English literature. His essay on "Bunyan" set thousands re-reading "Pilgrim's Progress." Whatever his faults may be, though he sometimes exaggerates or overstates his case, nevertheless, in the stimulating earnestness of his style, in his narrative power as an historian, in his originality and brilliancy as an historical essayist, he ranks with the masters of English prose.

Macaulay contributed his " Life of Samuel Johnson " to the " Encyclopedia Britannica " in 1856. Twenty-five years earlier he had published in the " Edinburgh Review " a critical essay on Croker's edition of Boswell's Johnson. No extended contrast or parallel between these two articles of Macaulay need here be drawn. However, the harsher judgments contained in the essay are toned down in the " Life ;" and generally, in the treatment of Johnson, the " Life " breathes a more tolerant and sympathetic spirit than does the article of 1831, which was, in fact, largely inspired by Macaulay's burning desire to expose the editorial blunders of his personal foe, Croker. The present " Life," moreover,—written at the culmination of Macaulay's powers and in the maturity of his style,—shows the brilliant essayist at his best. He has been taxed, however, with party bias and with inappreciation of the deeper elements of Johnson's character. Matthew Arnold, on the other hand, maintains that Macaulay, strong Whig though he was, had preëminent qualification, not only by virtue of his literary equipment, but also by many points of sympathetic resemblance to the Tory subject of his narrative, to deal with the theme of the great literary dictator of the eighteenth century.

In the "Life," as in the essay, Macaulay holds up to ridicule and scorn the character of Boswell, whose faults, like those of Cassius, seem to have been set in a notebook, conned, and learned by rote. His review of Boswell, however, is critical rather than biographical; and as the name and fame of "the painter" have become so closely linked with those of "the subject of the portrait," some brief summary of Boswell's life is appropriate here.

James Boswell (1740–95), born at Edinburgh, was the eldest son of Lord Auchinleck, a Scottish judge. He studied at Glasgow and Utrecht, and traveled extensively on the Continent. In Corsica he made the acquaintance of Pasquale Paoli, the leader of the revolt against Genoa, and, returning to England (1766), he posed as the champion of Corsican independence. Two years later he published his "Account of Corsica." He was admitted to the Scottish bar (1766), but never applied himself earnestly to the practice of his profession. He married his cousin, Margaret Montgomerie, in 1769.

Boswell's personality has made him one of the most amusing figures in English literary history. In his article of 1831, Macaulay says, "Boswell was one of the smallest men that ever lived. ... He was the laughingstock of the whole of that brilliant society which has owed to him the greater part of its fame. He was always laying himself at the feet of some eminent man, and begging to be spit upon and trampled upon. ... He exhibited himself at the Shakespeare Jubilee (1769) to all the crowd which filled Stratford-on-Avon, with a placard round his hat bearing the inscription of 'Corsica Boswell.' ... Servile and impertinent, shallow and pedantic, a bigot and a sot, bloated with family pride, and eternally blustering about the dignity of a born gentleman, yet stooping to be a talebearer, an eavesdropper, a common butt in the taverns of London, so curious to know everybody who was talked about, that, Tory and High-churchman as he was, he maneuvered . . . for an introduction to Tom Paine—so vain of the most childish distinctions, that, when he had been to court, he drove to the office where his book was printing, without changing his clothes, and summoned all the printer's devils to admire his new ruffles and sword."

Carlyle, in his essay on Johnson (1832), defended Boswell from the strictures of Macaulay. Indeed, what Macaulay stigmatizes as sycophancy, Carlyle deems a natural and honorable "hero worship" of Johnson.

It was in 1763, in the back parlor of Tom Davies, a London bookseller, that Boswell first met his hero. Johnson unexpectedly came into the shop. Davies, seeing him through the glass door, announced his approach to Boswell nearly in the words of Horatio to Hamlet: "Look, my lord! it comes;" and then and there the agitated Boswell was introduced to the "monarch of literature." "Recollecting Johnson's prejudice against the Scotch," writes Boswell, "I said to Davies, 'Don't tell where I come from!' —'From Scotland,' cried Davies roguishly. 'Mr. Johnson,' said I, 'I do indeed come from Scotland, but I cannot help it.' He retorted, 'That, sir, I find, is what a very great many of your countrymen cannot help.' The stroke stunned me a good deal."

In this way did Brobdingnag and Lilliput meet; and how this casual acquaintance ripened into the closest intimacy is known to all. Boswell "is only a bur," said Goldsmith, "flung at Johnson in sport, and he has the faculty of sticking."

Boswell's microscopic observation of his hero has been vividly described by Leslie Stephen: "When Johnson spoke, Boswell's eyes goggled with eagerness; he leant his ear almost on the doctor's shoulders; his mouth dropped open to catch every syllable; and he seemed to listen even to Johnson's breathings, as though they had some mystical significance."

In the painting of details, Boswell's prying curiosity stood him in good stead. Sir Isaac Newton, probably, was not more profoundly absorbed in his theory of gravitation than was "Bozzy," for the time being, in trying to ascertain (alas! in vain) the mysterious reasons that prompted Dr. Johnson to treasure up the orange peel, and refuse to wear a nightcap.

Vain and inquisitive as Boswell was, his perfect frankness and imperturbable good nature won him a welcome. Johnson called him "the best traveling companion in the world;" and the sage had an opportunity to test the amiable qualities of his faithful Achates during their famous tour of Scotland and the Hebrides (1773). Boswell published an account of this journey in 1785.

Boswell's masterpiece, "The Life of Samuel Johnson, LL.D.," appeared in 1791. Regarding the literary and artistic merits of this famous work, the weight of modern opinion is, that the biographer did not stumble upon his success by accident, but reaped it as the just reward of his systematic methods and unflagging zeal. He was uncrushable. "Sir," said Johnson to him on one occasion, "you have but two subjects, yourself and me. I am sick of both." Boswell, pocketing the rebuke, hid his diminished head, but continued none the less to gather his material for the biography, in which he has painted so vividly, not only the life of Johnson, but the life and manners of Johnson's time.

The main incidents of Johnson's career, grouped as they are by the masterly hand of Macaulay, need no further portrayal. The characteristics of Johnson, however, his place in literature, and his relation to his age, are here reviewed.

The thought and action of any period of history are necessarily closely allied; and only by the light of the times in which the famous dictionary maker lived can his prejudices and opinions be read aright. Accordingly one must place himself as far as possible amid Johnson's surroundings, with a sympathetic sense, moreover, of the literary and social conditions of the eighteenth century, of which, in many ways, the sage of Bolt Court was a vigorous embodiment.

In its social aspects Johnson's age was rough and unrefined. The prevailing coarseness of fashionable life is mirrored in the novels of Fielding and Smollett. The works of the shameless Aphra Behn were found on the toilet tables of the Belindas and Flirtillas of the day. Under the first two Georges, the passion for gambling reached its climax, fashionable ladies often playing for the highest stakes. "Beau Nash," the "King of Bath," where he presided in the famous pump room, was a professional gambler. "Even wise old Johnson regretted that he had never learned to play cards." The immorality of the court (up to the reign of George III.) was notorious; while the amusements of the populace were brutal in the extreme. The newspapers of 1730 contain an advertisement of "a mad bull, dressed up with fireworks, to be baited."

It was a time when men lived hard, and fought hard. In the field of debate and discussion, no quarter was given nor taken. The burly assertiveness and dogged courage that made Walpole premier were the prime requisites of the day. Of such a time, therefore, an aggressive and rugged character like Johnson is in no small measure typical. The age might trample upon the fastidious and delicate Gray; but it could not trample upon the rough-and-ready dictionary maker, who was famed as a hard hitter in debate, and who on one memorable occasion had knocked down a bookseller, one of the ogres of London, for his intolerable insolence. Few men, indeed, had the temerity to contend with Johnson. "There is no arguing with him," said Goldsmith; "for, if his pistol misses fire, he knocks you down with the butt of it."

The coarseness of the age, however, but brings into stronger relief the high moral tone of Johnson's character; nor did the prevalent skepticism of the early eighteenth century shake his firm and abiding religious faith.

Under the first two Georges, literature had a cheerless prospect. Walpole, famed as the Sir Visto of Pope and the Flimnap of Swift, despised reading; while George II., invoked as "Augustus" by poetical flattery, grew furious at the sight of a printed volume, and wasted little love on what he called "boetry" and "bainting." Patronage there was, to be sure, for political scribblers like Arnall, of whom the author of the "Dunciad" wrote:—

"Spirit of Arnall, aid me whilst I lie."

But the royal favor did little to foster a genuine love of letters.

Yet the years of Johnson's life (especially the first sixty years) belong to an era highly creative in English prose. In those memorable years appeared "Gulliver's Travels" (1729), with its pointed satire on the times of George I.; "Pamela" (1741), the first English domestic novel in the modern sense; Fielding's "Tom Jones" (1749); Smollett's delineations of the British tar, like Commodore Trunnion and Tom Bowling; Sterne's delightful creations of Uncle Toby and Corporal Trim in "Tristram Shandy"

(1760); Goldsmith's immortal "Vicar of Wakefield;" the histories of Hume and Robertson, and a portion of Gibbon's "Roman Empire;" the Wealth of Nations" (1776), that ranks "among the greatest of books;" and the magnificent speeches of Edmund Burke.

Johnson's connection with the production of Goldsmith's classic is a memorable incident in English literary history. One day (1764) "Goldy," as Johnson loved to call him, was arrested by his landlady for debt. Johnson, learning of his friend's sorry predicament, sent him a guinea, and then hastily proceeded to Goldsmith's lodgings. There he found that the guinea had been spent for a bottle of Madeira, in which his prodigal friend was drowning his sorrows. Without a word, Johnson solemnly corked the bottle, and locked it up. Then Goldsmith pulled from a drawer the manuscript of the "Vicar of Wakefield," which Johnson, after examination, took to a bookseller's (with whom he was influential), and sold for sixty pounds; and in this way was "Goldy" kept from the terrors of "the sponging house," and the story of Dr. Primrose launched on its long career of popularity.

Some influences of Johnson's age are plainly discernible in his literary style. The pompous Anglo-Latin diction of the "Rambler" expresses the renewed fondness for classical learning in his time, and the reaction in English prose against the simplicity of Addison. The faults of Johnson's early style (Johnsonese) are attributable in general to "a use of too big words, and too many of them," and in particular to an extravagant use of Latin derivatives and abstract terms; he employs antitheses even "when there is no opposition in the ideas expressed." The style of the "Rambler," however, differs much from that of his later years. The language of the "Lives of the Poets" (1777–81) is comparatively simple, and his conversation was racy with the plainest Anglo-Saxon.

If, however, Johnson's age was rich in pro**, it was poor in poetry. The "monarch of literature" lived between the Augustan age and the Victorian era. In his day the influences of the classical or Queen Anne school of poets were still predominant. There was no Wordsworth (1770–1850) to interpret Nature in her every word, or to sing "the still, sad music of humanity;" and so, as a rule, the early Georgian poetry is satirical or didactic. Johnson's "Vanity of Human Wishes" (1749) is written in the style of Pope; and he, moreover, only expressed the Augustan taste of the time in his bluntly avowed preference for Charing Cross and Fleet Street to all the beauties of nature.

Conservative as he was, then, Johnson had no appreciative sense of the coming revolution in English poetry,—the revolution that found an early expression in the poems of some of his contemporaries, "The Seasons" of Thomson, descriptive of natural scenery, and in the odes of Collins and Gray. Consequently, many of Johnson's literary judgments have been reversed in the present century.

Among the conspicuous examples of his mistaken criticism are the condemnatory opinions of Milton and Gray. The diction of Milton's "Lycidas" he deemed harsh, and the numbers unpleasing, while he styled Gray "a barren rascal." Yet in general Johnson bestowed high praise on the Puritan poet, and he did full justice to the best stanzas of Gray's "Elegy."

Johnson's place in literature is unique. He is best remembered by the story of his life and conversation. His wit and wisdom, preserved not only by Boswell, but also in the "Johnsoniana" of Mrs. Thrale (Piozzi), Tyers, Cradock, Madame d'Arblay, Hannah

More, and others, fill many entertaining and instructive pages. Ben Jonson, in his day and generation, had been a literary power; Dryden had had his throne, and Addison ("Atticus"), his "senate;" but no other man ever reigned supreme in the world of letters as did Dr. Johnson in the fullness of his fame. Long will the sage linger in our memories as the central figure in the intellectual combats and passages at arms associated with the names of the Literary Club and the Mitre Tavern.

Courage has been called the key to Johnson's character. His characteristic letter to the mighty Chesterfield is often quoted. Chesterfield, after long withholding his patronage from the struggling lexicographer, angled for the " Dedication " when the dictionary was coming out, and tried to smooth over Johnson's long-cherished resentment by graceful compliments.

" I have been lately informed by the proprietor of the ' World,' " writes Johnson, " that two papers in which my dictionary is recommended to the public were written by your lordship. To be so distinguished is an honor which, being very little accustomed to favors from the great, I know not well how to receive, or in what terms to acknowledge.

"When, upon some slight encouragement, I first visited your lordship, I was overpowered, like the rest of mankind, by the enchantment of your address, and could not forbear to wish that I might boast myself *le vainqueur du vainqueur de la terre,*[1] that I might obtain that regard for which I saw the world contending; but I found my attendance so little encouraged, that neither pride nor modesty would suffer me to continue it. When I had once addressed your lordship in public, I had exhausted all the arts of pleasing which a retired and uncourtly scholar can possess. I

---

[1] The conqueror of the conqueror of the earth.

had done all that I could; and no man is well pleased to have his all neglected, be it ever so little.

"Seven years, my lord, have now passed since I waited in your outward rooms, or was repulsed from your door; during which time I have been pushing on my work through difficulties of which it is useless to complain, and have brought it at last to the verge of publication, without one act of assistance, one word of encouragement, or one smile of favor. Such treatment I did not expect, for I never had a patron before.

"The shepherd in Virgil grew at last acquainted with Love, and found him a native of the rocks.

"Is not a patron, my lord, one who looks with unconcern on a man struggling for life in the water, and when he has reached ground encumbers him with help? The notice which you have been pleased to take of my labors, had it been early, had been kind; but it has been delayed till I am indifferent, and cannot enjoy it; till I am solitary, and cannot impart it; till I am known, and do not want it. I hope it is no very cynical asperity not to confess obligations where no benefit has been received, or to be unwilling that the public should consider me as owing that to a patron which Providence has enabled me to do for myself."

This famous letter dealt "patronage" a fatal blow.

Johnson's prejudices are far-famed. Yet "that Jacobitism, Church of Englandism, hatred of the Scotch, belief in witches, and such like,—what were they but the ordinary beliefs of well-doing, well-meaning provincial Englishmen in his day?" He was called a "good hater;" but he lived in an era of "good haters." In the earlier years of his life, to be sure, a spirit of apathy or cold indifference, akin to the studied avoidance of the emotional in Augustan literature, had characterized political and

2

religious thought; but there succeeded a period of intense earnestness in national life,—the days of Pitt and Clive, Wesley and Whitefield. "Never before," writes Green, in commenting upon the year 1759, "had England played so great a .part in the history of mankind." Peace, moreover, as well as war, had its famous victories; and the Methodist revival "changed after a while the whole tone of English society."

Johnson, then, represents the *conservative* side of his century. The political corruption under the Whigs, and the parliamentary bribery rampant during the leadership of Walpole, naturally tended to confirm Johnson's inherited Tory principles; nor is it surprising that he could not adjust the opinions and sympathies of his old age to more liberal tendencies or progressive movements.

Of Whitefield's stirring eloquence he said, "His popularity is chiefly owing to the peculiarity of his manner. He would be followed by crowds, were he to wear a nightcap in the pulpit, or were he to preach from a tree."

Johnson, however, outlived many of his prejudices. His hatred of the Scotch became a mere joke; and some of his closest intimates were "Whig dogs." The stout old Tory even condescended once to dine with Jack Wilkes, that notorious profligate, demagogue, and infidel.

Johnson was a "clubable" man; and his characterization of a tavern chair as the throne of human felicity signified his enjoyment of intellectual companionship, with "its feast of reason and flow of soul." As Garrick put it, Johnson "fairly shook laughter out of you." He enjoyed romping games; and it must have been rare sport to see the big-bodied philosopher, in his moments of recreation, playing hop, step, and jump, in which game he was reputed to be expert.

In figure Johnson was tall and well-formed. He possessed great physical strength; and many instances of his fearlessness are recorded. Thackeray pictures him as "that great, awkward, pock-marked, snuff-colored man, swaying to and fro as he walks."

He generally wore a suit of plain brown clothes, with twisted hair buttons of the same color, a large, bushy, grayish wig, and black worsted stockings. Upon his tour in Scotland he wore a wide greatcoat, with pockets in it almost big enough to hold the two volumes of his folio dictionary. In his time, men of rank and fashion displayed the most gorgeous attire. "Goldy's" absorbing passion for brilliant waistcoats is well known. Wilkes generally arrayed himself in a scarlet or green suit edged with gold. Johnson himself, in his later years, became more careful in his dress, and, yielding to the persuasive influences of Mrs. Thrale, adorned his coat with metal buttons, and his shoes with silver buckles.

The life of Samuel Johnson was "the victorious battle of a free, true man." His name is likely to be remembered "as long as the English language is spoken in any quarter of the globe."

SAMUEL JOHNSON.

SAMUEL JOHNSON, one of the most eminent English writers of the eighteenth century, was the son of Michael Johnson, who was, at the beginning of that century, a magistrate of Lichfield, and a bookseller of great note in the midland counties. Michael's abilities and attainments seem to have been considerable. He was so well acquainted with the contents of the volumes which he exposed to sale, that the country rectors of Staffordshire and Worcestershire thought him an oracle on points of learning. Between him and the clergy, indeed, there was a strong religious and political sympathy. He was a zealous churchman, and, though he had qualified himself for municipal office by taking the oaths to the sovereigns in possession, was to the last a Jacobite [1] in heart. At his house, a house which is still pointed out to every traveler who visits Lichfield, Samuel was born on the 18th of September, 1709. In the child, the physical, intellectual, and moral peculiarities which afterwards distinguished the man were plainly discernible,—great muscular strength accompanied by much awkwardness and many infirmities; great quickness of parts, with a morbid propensity to sloth and procrastination; a kind and generous heart, with a gloomy and irritable temper. He had inherited from his ancestors a scrofulous taint, which it was beyond the power of medicine to remove. His parents were weak enough to believe that the royal

---

[1] An adherent of James II., or of his descendants; from the Latin *Jacobus* (James).

touch was a specific for this malady.[1] In his third year he was
taken up to London, inspected by the court surgeon, prayed over
by the court chaplains, and stroked and presented with a piece
of gold by Queen Anne. One of his earliest recollections was
that of a stately lady in a diamond stomacher and a long black
hood. Her hand was applied in vain. The boy's features, which
were originally noble and not irregular, were distorted by his
malady. His cheeks were deeply scarred. He lost for a time
the sight of one eye, and he saw but very imperfectly with the
other. But the force of his mind overcame every impediment.
Indolent as he was, he acquired knowledge with such ease and
rapidity, that at every school to which he was sent he was soon
the best scholar. From sixteen to eighteen he resided at home,
and was left to his own devices. He learned much at this time,
though his studies were without guidance and without plan. He
ransacked his father's shelves, dipped into a multitude of books,
read what was interesting, and passed over what was dull. An
ordinary lad would have acquired little or no useful knowledge in
such a way; but much that was dull to ordinary lads was interesting to Samuel. He read little Greek; for his proficiency in
that language was not such that he could take much pleasure in
the masters of Attic[2] poetry and eloquence. But he had left
school a good Latinist, and he soon acquired, in the large and
miscellaneous library of which he now had the command, an extensive knowledge of Latin literature. That Augustan[3] delicacy
of taste which is the boast of the great public schools of England,
he never possessed. But he was early familiar with some classical writers who were quite unknown to the best scholars in the

---

[1] This superstition was widespread in Queen Anne's reign (1702–14).
The newspapers of the time record that in one day — March 30, 1712 — two
hundred persons were touched by the Queen.

[2] Athenian, the most highly cultivated dialect of the Greek tongue.

[3] Under Emperor Augustus (died, A.D. 14), Roman literature reached its
highest point. The period of Queen Anne has been styled " the Augustan
age " of English literature.

sixth form at Eton.[1] He was peculiarly attracted by the works of the great restorers of learning.[2] Once, while searching for some apples, he found a huge folio volume of Petrarch's [3] works. The name excited his curiosity, and he eagerly devoured hundreds of pages. Indeed, the diction and versification of his own Latin compositions show that he had paid at least as much attention to modern copies from the antique as to the original models.

While he was thus irregularly educating himself, his family was sinking into hopeless poverty. Old Michael Johnson was much better qualified to pore upon books, and to talk about them, than to trade in them. His business declined: his debts increased; it was with difficulty that the daily expenses of his household were defrayed. It was out of his power to support his son at either university;[4] but a wealthy neighbor offered assistance, and, in reliance on promises which proved to be of very little value, Samuel was entered at Pembroke College, Oxford. When the young scholar presented himself to the rulers of that society, they were amazed not more by his ungainly figure and eccentric manners than by the quantity of extensive and curious information which he had picked up during many months of desultory, but not unprofitable study. On the first day of his residence, he surprised his teachers by quoting Macrobius;[5] and one of the most learned

---

[1] One of the famous schools of England. Walpole, Gray, Shelley, Fox, Canning, and the Duke of Wellington were educated at Eton.

[2] A revival of learning and classical study marked the great intellectual movement of the fourteenth, fifteenth, and sixteenth centuries. The text alludes to famous scholars of the Renaissance, like Petrarch, Politian, Erasmus, and Sir Thomas More.

[3] A celebrated Italian poet (1304-74).

[4] Oxford or Cambridge, the two great English universities. Christ Church, one of the greatest and most fashionable colleges of Oxford, was established by Henry VIII. Pembroke College was founded in 1624; its library contains many memorials of Johnson.

[5] Roman grammarian (beginning of fifth century), and author of a series of essays.

among them declared that he had never known a freshman of equal attainments.

At Oxford, Johnson resided during about three years. He was poor, even to raggedness; and his appearance excited a mirth and a pity which were equally intolerable to his haughty spirit. He was driven from the quadrangle of Christ Church by the sneering looks which the members of that aristocratical society cast at the holes in his shoes. Some charitable person placed a new pair at his door; but he spurned them away in a fury. Distress made him, not servile, but reckless and ungovernable. No opulent gentleman commoner,[1] panting for one and twenty, could have treated the academical authorities with more gross disrespect. The needy scholar was generally to be seen under the gate of Pembroke, a gate now adorned with his effigy, haranguing a circle of lads, over whom, in spite of his tattered gown and dirty linen, his wit and audacity gave him an undisputed ascendency. In every mutiny against the discipline of the college, he was the ringleader. Much was pardoned, however, to a youth so highly distinguished by abilities and acquirements. He had early made himself known by turning Pope's " Messiah "[2] into Latin verse. The style and rhythm, indeed, were not exactly Virgilian;[3] but the translation found many admirers, and was read with pleasure by Pope himself.

The time drew near at which Johnson would, in the ordinary

[1] A student in some English colleges (Oxford and Winchester), who pays for his commons, and who is not, like a fellow, dependent on the foundation for support. There grew up at Oxford, students of many ranks, — noblemen, gentlemen commoners, fellow commoners, servitors; but these grades are now practically obsolete, students being distinguished as " commoners " or " scholars " (students " on the foundation ").

[2] A sacred eclogue by Alexander Pope (1688–1744), in imitation of Virgil's Pollio, first published in the Spectator. It is written in rhyming couplets. " In reading several passages of the prophet Isaiah which foretell the coming of Christ," said Pope, " I could not but observe a remarkable parity between many of the thoughts and those in the Pollio of Virgil."

[3] Virgil (70–19 B.C.) was a celebrated Roman poet of the Augustan age; author of Eclogues, Georgics, and the Æneid.

course of things, have become a bachelor of arts; but he was at the end of his resources. Those promises of support on which he had relied had not been kept. His family could do nothing for him. His debts to Oxford tradesmen were small indeed, yet larger than he could pay. In the autumn of 1731 he was under the necessity of quitting the university without a degree. In the following winter his father died. The old man left but a pittance; and of that pittance almost the whole was appropriated to the support of his widow. The property to which Samuel succeeded amounted to no more than twenty pounds.

His life, during the thirty years which followed, was one hard struggle with poverty. The misery of that struggle needed no aggravation, but was aggravated by the sufferings of an unsound body and an unsound mind. Before the young man left the university, his hereditary malady had broken forth in a singularly cruel form. He had become an incurable hypochondriac. He said long after, that he had been mad all his life, or at least not perfectly sane; and, in truth, eccentricities less strange than his have often been thought grounds sufficient for absolving felons and for setting aside wills. His grimaces, his gestures,[1] his mutterings, sometimes diverted and sometimes terrified people who did not know him. At a dinner table he would, in a fit of absence, stoop down and twitch off a lady's shoe. He would amaze a drawing-room by suddenly ejaculating a clause of the Lord's Prayer. He would conceive an unintelligible aversion to a particular alley, and perform a great circuit rather than see the hateful place. He would set his heart on touching every post in the streets through which he walked. If by any chance he missed a post, he would go back a hundred yards, and repair the omission. Under the influence of his disease, his senses became morbidly torpid, and his imagination morbidly active. At one

---

[1] Of these motions or tricks of Dr. Johnson, Sir Joshua Reynolds said, "He could sit motionless, when he was told to do so, as well as any other man. My opinion is, that it proceeded from a habit, which he had indulged himself in, of accompanying his thoughts with certain untoward actions."

time he would stand poring on the town clock without being
able to tell the hour. At another, he would distinctly hear his
mother, who was many miles off, calling him by his name. But
this was not the worst. A deep melancholy took possession of
him, and gave a dark tinge to all his views of human nature and
of human destiny. Such wretchedness as he endured has driven
many men to shoot themselves or drown themselves. But he
was under no temptation to commit suicide. He was sick of
life, but he was afraid of death; and he shuddered at every sight
or sound which reminded him of the inevitable hour. In religion
he found but little comfort during his long and frequent fits of
dejection; for his religion partook of his own character. The
light from heaven shone on him indeed, but not in a direct line,
or with its own pure splendor. The rays had to struggle through
a disturbing medium: they reached him refracted, dulled, and
discolored by the thick gloom which had settled on his soul; and,
though they might be sufficiently clear to guide him, were too dim
to cheer him.

With such infirmities of body and of mind, this celebrated man
was left, at two and twenty, to fight his way through the world.
He remained during about five years in the midland counties.
At Lichfield, his birthplace and his early home, he had inherited
some friends, and acquired others. He was kindly noticed by
Henry Hervey,[1] a gay officer of noble family, who happened
to be quartered there. Gilbert Walmesley,[2] registrar of the
ecclesiastical court[3] of the diocese,—a man of distinguished
parts, learning, and knowledge of the world,—did himself honor
by patronizing the young adventurer, whose repulsive person,
unpolished manners, and squalid garb, moved many of the petty
aristocracy of the neighborhood to laughter or to disgust. At

---

[1] The Hon. Henry Hervey, third son of the first Earl of Bristol: his
eldest brother was Pope's Lord Fanny (see Note 4, p. 27).

[2] Author (died, 1751) of many Latin verses, translated in the Gentleman's
Magazine.

[3] The Prerogative Court.

Lichfield, however, Johnson could find no way of earning a
livelihood. He became usher of a grammar school in Leicestershire; he resided as a humble companion in the house of a
country gentleman; but a life of dependence was insupportable
to his haughty spirit. He repaired to Birmingham, and there
earned a few guineas by literary drudgery. In that town he
printed a translation, little noticed at the time, and long forgotten, of a Latin book about Abyssinia.[1] He then put forth
proposals for publishing by subscription the poems of Politian,[2]
with notes containing a history of modern Latin verse; but subscriptions did not come in, and the volume never appeared.

While leading this vagrant and miserable life, Johnson fell in
love. The object of his passion was Mrs. Elizabeth Porter, a
widow who had children as old as himself. To ordinary specta-
tors, the lady appeared to be a short, fat, coarse woman, painted
half an inch thick, dressed in gaudy colors, and fond of exhibit-
ing provincial airs and graces which were not exactly those of
the Queensberrys[3] and Lepels.[4] To Johnson, however, whose
passions were strong, whose eyesight was too weak to distinguish
ceruse from natural bloom, and who had seldom or never been
in the same room with a woman of real fashion, his Titty, as he
called her, was the most beautiful, graceful, and accomplished of
her sex. That his admiration was unfeigned cannot be doubted,
for she was as poor as himself. She accepted, with a readiness
which did her little honor, the addresses of a suitor who might
have been her son. The marriage, however, in spite of occasional
wranglings, proved happier than might have been expected. The

---

[1] Translation and abridgment of a Voyage to Abyssinia, by Father Lobo,
a Portuguese priest (1593-1678).

[2] A Florentine poet and scholar (1454-94); author of poems in Latin and
Italian.

[3] Catherine Hyde (died, 1777), Duchess of Queensberry, a celebrated
beauty, was the eccentric friend of Gay. See Letters of Horace Walpole
(to Conway, June 8, 1747).

[4] A friend of Pope. She married Lord John Hervey (1696-1743), who
wrote Memoirs of the Reign of George II. (see Thackeray's George II.).

lover continued to be under the illusions of the wedding day till the lady died, in her sixty-fourth year. On her monument he placed an inscription extolling the charms of her person and of her manners; and when, long after her decease, he had occasion to mention her, he exclaimed, with a tenderness half ludicrous, half pathetic, " Pretty creature ! "

His marriage made it necessary for him to exert himself more strenuously than he had hitherto done. He took a house in the neighborhood of his native town, and advertised for pupils. But eighteen months passed away; and only three pupils came to his academy. Indeed, his appearance was so strange, and his temper so violent, that his schoolroom must have resembled an ogre's den. Nor was the tawdry painted grandmother whom he called his Titty, well qualified to make provision for the comfort of young gentlemen. David Garrick,[1] who was one of the pupils, used many years later to throw the best company of London into convulsions of laughter by mimicking the endearments of this extraordinary pair.

At length Johnson, in the twenty-eighth year of his age, determined to seek his fortune in the capital as a literary adventurer. He set out with a few guineas, three acts of the tragedy of " Irene "[2] in manuscript, and two or three letters of introduction from his friend Walmesley.

Never since literature became a calling in England had it been a less gainful calling than at the time when Johnson took up his residence in London. In the preceding generation, a writer of eminent merit was sure to be munificently rewarded by the government. The least that he could expect was a pension or a sinecure place; and, if he showed any aptitude for politics, he

---

[1] The celebrated actor (1716–79). He was before all a Shakespearean actor, and (according to Lecky) did more than any other man to extend the popularity of Shakespeare. In 1741 he made his appearance in the character of Richard III. Gray, in a letter (1741), says, " Did I tell you about Mr. Garrick that the town are horn-mad after ? There are a dozen dukes of a night at Goodman's Fields [Theater] sometimes."

[2] See p. 40.

might hope to be a member of Parliament, a lord of the treasury, an ambassador, a secretary of state.[1] It would be easy, on the other hand, to name several writers[2] of the nineteenth century, of whom the least successful has received forty thousand pounds from the booksellers. But Johnson entered on his vocation in the most dreary part of the dreary interval which separated two ages of prosperity. Literature had ceased to flourish under the patronage of the great, and had not begun to flourish under the patronage of the public. One man of letters, indeed, Pope, had acquired by his pen what was then considered as a handsome fortune,[3] and lived on a footing of equality with nobles and ministers of state. But this was a solitary exception. Even an author whose reputation was established and whose works were popular—such an author as Thomson,[4] whose " Seasons " were in every library ; such an author as Fielding,[5] whose " Pasquin " had had a greater run than any drama since the " Beggar's Opera "[6]—was sometimes glad to obtain, by pawning his best coat, the means of dining on tripe at a cookshop underground, where he could wipe his hands, after his greasy meal, on the back of a Newfoundland dog. It is easy, therefore, to imagine what humiliations and privations must have awaited the novice who had still to earn a name. One of the publishers to whom Johnson applied for employment measured with a scornful eye

[1] In the executive department of the English Government, the Treasury Board consists of four lords of the treasury and a chancellor of the exchequer. To the first lord of the treasury are usually assigned the duties of the prime minister. There are five secretaries of state ; namely, for the home, foreign, colonial, war, and Indian departments.

[2] Scott and Byron.

[3] Pope's translation of Homer brought him about nine thousand pounds.

[4] James Thomson (1700–48). See Introduction.

[5] Henry Fielding (1707–54), one of the greatest of English novelists ; author of Tom Jones. Pasquin (1736) is a dramatic satire.

[6] An English ballad opera (1728) by John Gay (1688–1732). It was written to ridicule the Italian operatic style ; and its chief characters, highwaymen and pickpockets, are a satire on the corrupt statesmen of the day.

that athletic though uncouth frame, and exclaimed, "You had better get a porter's knot,[1] and carry trunks." Nor was the advice bad; for a porter was likely to be as plentifully fed and as comfortably lodged as a poet.

Some time appears to have elapsed before Johnson was able to form any literary connection from which he could expect more than bread for the day which was passing over him. He never forgot the generosity with which Hervey, who was now residing in London, relieved his wants during this time of trial. "Harry Hervey," said the old philosopher many years later, "was a vicious man; but he was very kind to me. If you call a dog Hervey, I shall love him." At Hervey's table, Johnson sometimes enjoyed feasts which were made more agreeable by contrast. But in general he dined, and thought that he dined well, on sixpennyworth of meat and a pennyworth of bread at an alehouse near Drury Lane.[2]

The effect of the privations and sufferings which he endured at this time was discernible to the last in his temper and his deportment. His manners had never been courtly. They now became almost savage. Being frequently under the necessity of wearing shabby coats and dirty shirts, he became a confirmed sloven. Being often very hungry when he sat down to his meals, he contracted a habit of eating with ravenous greediness. Even to the end of his life, and even at the tables of the great, the sight of food affected him as it affects wild beasts and birds of prey. His taste in cookery, formed in subterranean ordinaries[3] and *alamode* beefshops, was far from delicate. Whenever he was so fortunate as to have near him a hare that had been kept too long, or a meat pie made with rancid butter, he gorged himself with such violence, that his veins swelled and the moisture broke out

[1] "A pad for supporting burdens on the head."

[2] A London street communicating with the Strand; near it, on Russell Street, is the celebrated Drury Lane Theater, first opened in 1663.

[3] "Ordinary," i.e., "a place of eating established at a certain price."— JOHNSON: *Dictionary.*

on his forehead. The affronts which his poverty emboldened stupid and low-minded men to offer to him, would have broken a mean spirit into sycophancy, but made him rude even to ferocity. Unhappily, the insolence, which, while it was defensive, was pardonable and in some sense respectable, accompanied him into societies where he was treated with courtesy and kindness. He was repeatedly provoked into striking those who had taken liberties with him. All the sufferers, however, were wise enough to abstain from talking about their beatings, except Osborne, the most rapacious and brutal of booksellers, who proclaimed everywhere that he had been knocked down by the huge fellow whom he had hired to puff the Harleian Library.[1]

About a year after Johnson had begun to reside in London, he was fortunate enough to obtain regular employment from Cave,[2] an enterprising and intelligent bookseller, who was proprietor and editor of the "Gentleman's Magazine." That journal, just entering on the ninth year of its long existence, was the only periodical work in the kingdom which then had what would now be called a large circulation. It was, indeed, the chief source of parliamentary intelligence. It was not then safe, even during a recess, to publish an account of the proceedings of either House without some disguise. Cave, however, ventured to entertain his readers with what he called "Reports of the Debates of the Senate of Lilliput."[3] France was Blefuscu; London was Mildendo; pounds were sprugs; the Duke of Newcastle[4] was the Nardac secretary of state; Lord Hardwicke[5] was the Hugo Hickrad; and William Pulteney[6] was Wingul Pulnub. To write the speeches was, dur-

---

[1] The celebrated collection of books made by the Earl of Oxford (Henry Harley), purchased by Osborne for thirteen thousand pounds (see Note 2, p. 59).   [2] Edward Cave (1691-1754).

[3] The name is taken from Swift's Gulliver's Travels.

[4] A famous Whig statesman (1693-1768), secretary of state and premier : he formed a coalition with Pitt (1757).   See Macaulay's Chatham.

[5] Whig statesman (1690-1764) : as lord chancellor he won a high reputation.

[6] Famous Whig leader (1684-1764), at first a friend of Walpole, but afterward the head of the faction called " the Patriots ; " created Earl of Bath.

ing several years, the business of Johnson. He was generally furnished with notes—meager indeed, and inaccurate—of what had been said; but sometimes he had to find arguments and eloquence, both for the ministry and for the opposition. He was himself a Tory,[1] not from rational conviction,—for his serious opinion was, that one form of government was just as good or as bad as another,—but from mere passion, such as inflamed the Capulets against the Montagues,[2] or the Blues of the Roman circus against the Greens.[3] In his infancy he had heard so much talk about the villainies of the Whigs[4] and the dangers of the Church, that he had become a furious partisan when he could scarcely speak. Before he was three, he had insisted on being taken to hear Sacheverell[5] preach at Lichfield Cathedral, and had listened to the sermon with as much respect, and probably with as much intelligence, as any Staffordshire squire in the congregation. The work which had been begun in the nursery had been completed by the university. Oxford, when Johnson resided there, was the most Jacobitical place in England; and Pembroke was one of the most Jacobitical colleges in Oxford. The prejudices which he brought up to London were scarcely less absurd than those of his own Tom Tempest.[6] Charles II. and James II.[7] were two of the best kings that ever reigned.

---

[1] The Tories were the peace party in Queen Anne's reign, and had a strong ally in the Church. During Johnson's earlier years (1712–42) the Whigs ruled England.

[2] In Shakespeare's Romeo and Juliet, the families of the two lovers, the Montagues and the Capulets, cherish an hereditary feud.

[3] For an account of the circus factions at Constantinople, see Gibbon's Roman Empire, chap. xli.

[4] Of the two great political parties, the Whigs were the more liberal. They defended the revolution of 1688, and favored the Hanoverian succession.

[5] Dr. Henry Sacheverell (1672–1724) a High-church divine who preached in severe terms against the Whig administration. He was impeached (1710), and suspended from office for three years.

[6] A bigoted and noisy partisan. For the character, see Idler No. 10.

[7] Charles II. reigned 1660–85; and James II., 1685–88.

Laud,[1] a poor creature who never did, said, or wrote anything indicating more than the ordinary capacity of an old woman, was a prodigy of parts and learning, over whose tomb Art and Genius [2] still continued to weep. Hampden[3] deserved no more honorable name than that of "the zealot of rebellion." Even the ship money,[4] condemned not less decidedly by Falkland [5] and Clarendon [6] than by the bitterest Roundheads,[7] Johnson would not pronounce to have been an unconstitutional impost. Under a government the mildest that had ever been known in the world, under a government, which allowed to the people an unprecedented liberty of speech and action, he fancied that he was a slave; he assailed the ministry with obloquy which refuted itself, and regretted the lost freedom and happiness of those golden days in which a writer who had taken but one-tenth part of the license allowed to him would have been pilloried, mangled with the shears, whipped at the cart's tail, and flung into a noisome dungeon to die. He hated dissenters and stockjobbers, the excise and the army, septennial parliaments and continental connections. He long had an aversion to the Scotch, an aversion of which he could not remember the commencement, but which, he owned, had probably originated in his abhorrence of the conduct of the nation during the Great Rebellion.[8] It is easy to guess in what manner debates on great party questions were likely to be re-

1 Archbishop Laud (1573-1645), the persecutor of the Puritans. He was impeached and executed.

2 "Around his tomb let Art and Genius weep." — *Vanity of Human Wishes,* line 173.

3 John Hampden (1594-1643), celebrated leader of the patriotic party against Charles I.

4 An arbitrary tax imposed by Charles I., first introduced in 1634. The tax was levied on the whole kingdom, and the money raised was expended on the navy.

5 A Royalist leader (1610-43) in the civil war.

6 A Royalist statesman (1608-74), author of a history of the civil war.

7 A name given in derision by the Royalists to the Puritans and Independents.

8 The civil war against Charles I., begun in 1642.

ported by a man whose judgment was so much disordered by
party spirit. A show of fairness was, indeed, necessary to the
prosperity of the magazine. But Johnson long afterwards owned,
that, though he had saved appearances, he had taken care that
the Whig dogs should not have the best of it; and, in fact,
every passage which has lived, every passage which bears the
marks of his higher faculties, is put into the mouth of some
member of the opposition.

A few weeks after Johnson had entered on these obscure
labors, he published a work which at once placed him high among
the writers of his age. It is probable that what he had suffered
during his first year in London had often reminded him of some
parts of that noble poem in which Juvenal [1] had described the
misery and degradation of a needy man of letters, lodged among
the pigeons' nests in the tottering garrets which overhung
the streets of Rome. Pope's admirable imitations of Horace's [2]
" Satires " and " Epistles " had recently appeared, were in every
hand, and were by many readers thought superior to the originals.
What Pope had done for Horace, Johnson aspired to do for
Juvenal. The enterprise was bold, and yet judicious. For between Johnson and Juvenal there was much in common,—much
more, certainly, than between Pope and Horace.

Johnson's " London " appeared without his name in May, 1738.
He received only ten guineas for this stately and vigorous poem ;
but the sale was rapid, and the success complete. A second
edition was required within a week. Those small critics who
are always desirous to lower established reputations, ran about
proclaiming that the anonymous satirist was superior to Pope in
Pope's own peculiar department of literature. It ought to be
remembered, to the honor of Pope, that he joined heartily in .
the applause with which the appearance of a rival genius was

[1] A famous Roman satirist (about A.D. 60–140). The allusion is to his
Third Satire.

[2] A famous poet (65–8 B.C.), whose odes, epistles, and satires show the
Latin tongue in its perfection. Pope's Moral Essays and Satires are Horatian.

welcomed. He made inquiries about the author of "London." Such a man, he said, could not long be concealed. The name was soon discovered; and Pope, with great kindness, exerted himself to obtain an academical degree, and the mastership of a grammar school, for the poor young poet. The attempt failed, and Johnson remained a bookseller's hack.

It does not appear that these two men—the most eminent writer of the generation which was going out, and the most eminent writer of the generation which was coming in—ever saw each other. They lived in very different circles, one surrounded by dukes and earls, the other by starving pamphleteers and index makers. Among Johnson's associates at this time may be mentioned Boyse,[1] who, when his shirts were pledged, scrawled Latin verses, sitting up in bed with his arms through two holes in his blankets, who composed very respectable sacred poetry when he was sober, and who was at last run over by a hackney coach when he was drunk; Hoole,[2] surnamed the metaphysical tailor, who, instead of attending to his measures, used to trace geometrical diagrams on the board where he sat cross-legged; and the penitent impostor, George Psalmanazar,[3] who, after poring all day, in a humble lodging, on the folios of Jewish rabbis and Christian fathers, indulged himself at night with literary and theological conversation at an alehouse in the city. But the most remarkable of the persons with whom at this time Johnson consorted, was Richard Savage,[4] an earl's son, a shoemaker's

---

[1] Samuel Boyse (1708–49), a forgotten literary drudge.

[2] John Hoole (1727–1803), the translator of Tasso and Ariosto, received part of his education in Grub Street, being taught by his uncle, "Hoole the tailor," who is here alluded to.

[3] The assumed name of a literary impostor (about 1679–1763), who pretended to be a native of Formosa, and wrote a fictitious account of that island (1704), and afterwards applied himself to the study of theology. He is mentioned in *Humphry Clinker.*

[4] Author of the *Wanderer* (born, 1698; died, 1743): his poetical works are now forgotten. He was reputed to be the illegitimate son of the Countess of Macclesfield.

apprentice, who had seen life in all its forms, who had feasted among blue ribbands in St. James's Square,[1] and had lain with fifty pounds' weight of irons on his legs in the condemned ward of Newgate.[2] This man had, after many vicissitudes of fortune, sunk at last into abject and hopeless poverty. His pen had failed him. His patrons had been taken away by death, or estranged by the riotous profusion with which he squandered their bounty, and the ungrateful insolence with which he rejected their advice. He now lived by begging. He dined on venison and champagne whenever he had been so fortunate as to borrow a guinea. If his questing had been unsuccessful, he appeased the rage of hunger with some scraps of broken meat, and lay down to rest under the piazza of Covent Garden[3] in warm weather, and in cold weather as near as he could get to the furnace of a glasshouse. Yet, in his misery, he was still an agreeable companion. He had an inexhaustible store of anecdotes about that gay and brilliant world from which he was now an outcast. He had observed the great men of both parties in hours of careless relaxation, had seen the leaders of opposition without the mask of patriotism, and had heard the prime minister roar with laughter, and tell stories not overdecent. During some months, Savage lived in the closest familiarity with Johnson; and then the friends parted, not without tears. Johnson remained in London to drudge for Cave. Savage went to the west of England, lived there as he had lived everywhere, and in 1743 died, penniless and heartbroken, in Bristol jail.

Soon after his death, while the public curiosity was strongly excited about his extraordinary character and his not less extraordinary adventures, a life of him appeared, widely different from

[1] Not far from St. James's Palace, for many years the most fashionable square in London. "Blue ribbands" stands by metonymy for members of the Order of the Garter.

[2] A prison for felons; destroyed and rebuilt several times.

[3] In Bow Street, Covent Garden, a square and marketplace in London, stands the theater of the same name.

the catchpenny lives of eminent men which were then a staple article of manufacture in Grub Street.[1] The style was, indeed, deficient in ease and variety; and the writer was evidently too partial to the Latin element of our language. But the little work, with all its faults, was a masterpiece. No finer specimen of literary biography existed in any language, living or dead; and a discerning critic might have confidently predicted that the author was destined to be the founder of a new school of English eloquence.

The " Life of Savage " was anonymous; but it was well known in literary circles that Johnson was the writer. During the three years which followed, he produced no important work; but he was not, and indeed could not be, idle. The fame of his abilities and learning continued to grow. Warburton [2] pronounced him a man of parts and genius; and the praise of Warburton was then no light thing. Such was Johnson's reputation, that in 1747 several eminent booksellers combined to employ him in the arduous work of preparing a " Dictionary of the English Language," in two folio volumes. The sum which they agreed to pay him was only fifteen hundred guineas; and out of this sum he had to pay several poor men of letters who assisted him in the humbler parts of his task.

The Prospectus of the Dictionary he addressed to the Earl of Chesterfield.[3] Chesterfield had long been celebrated for the politeness of his manners, the brilliancy of his wit, and the delicacy of his taste. He was acknowledged to be the finest speaker in the House of Lords. He had recently governed Ireland, at a momentous conjuncture, with eminent firmness, wisdom,

---

[1] " Originally the name of a street in Moorfields in London, much inhabited by writers of small histories, dictionaries, and temporary poems; whence any mean production is called *grubstreet.*" — JOHNSON: *Dictionary.* Grubstreet authors were satirized by Pope in the Dunciad.

[2] William Warburton (1698-1779), Bishop of Gloucester: a learned critic.

[3] Politician, orator, and man of fashion (1694-1773). He was renowned as a model of politeness, and his Letters to his son were accepted in his time as a manual of conduct.

and humanity; and he had since become secretary of state. He
received Johnson's homage with the most winning affability, and
requited it with a few guineas, bestowed, doubtless, in a very
graceful manner, but was by no means desirous to see all his
carpets blackened with the London mud, and his soups and wines
thrown to right and left over the gowns of fine ladies and the
waistcoats of fine gentlemen, by an absent, awkward scholar, who
gave strange starts, and uttered strange growls, who dressed like
a scarecrow, and ate like a cormorant. During some time, Johnson continued to call on his patron, but, after being repeatedly
told by the porter that his lordship was not at home, took the
hint, and ceased to present himself at the inhospitable door.

Johnson had flattered himself that he should have completed
his Dictionary by the end of 1750; but it was not till 1755 that
he at length gave his huge volumes to the world. During the
seven years which he passed in the drudgery of penning definitions, and marking quotations for transcription, he sought for relaxation in literary labor of a more agreeable kind. In 1749 he
published the "Vanity of Human Wishes," an excellent imitation
of the Tenth Satire of Juvenal. It is in truth not easy to say
whether the palm belongs to the ancient or to the modern poet.
The couplets [1] in which the fall of Wolsey [2] is described, though
lofty and sonorous, are feeble when compared with the wonderful
lines [3] which bring before us all Rome in tumult on the day of

[1] Lines 99-128.
[2] Thomas Wolsey (1471-1530), cardinal and prime minister of Henry VIII.
[3] Lines 56-80 (Gifford's translation): —

"The statues, tumbled down,
Are dragged by hooting thousands through the town;
The brazen cars, torn rudely from the yoke,
And with the blameless steeds to shivers broke. —
Then roar the fires! the sooty artist blows,
And all Sejanus in the furnace glows.
  .   .   .   .
"Crown all your doors with bay, triumphant bay!
Sacred to Jove, the milk-white victim slay;
For lo! where great Sejanus by the throng —
A joyful spectacle! — is dragged along."

the fall of Sejanus,[1] the laurels on the doorposts, the white bull
stalking towards the Capitol, the statues rolling down from their
pedestals, the flatterers of the disgraced minister running to see
him dragged with a hook through the streets, and to have a kick
at his carcass before it is hurled into the Tiber. It must be
owned, too, that in the concluding passage the Christian moralist
has not made the most of his advantages, and has fallen decidedly short of the sublimity of his Pagan model. On the other
hand, Juvenal's Hannibal[2] must yield to Johnson's Charles;[3]
and Johnson's vigorous and pathetic enumeration[4] of the miseries
of a literary life must be allowed to be superior to Juvenal's
lamentation over the fate of Demosthenes[5] and Cicero.[6]

For the copyright of the " Vanity of Human Wishes," Johnson
received only fifteen guineas.

A few days after the publication of this poem, his tragedy,
begun many years before, was brought on the stage. His pupil,
David Garrick, had in 1741 made his appearance on a humble
stage in Goodman's Fields, had at once risen to the first place
among actors, and was now, after several years of almost uninter-
rupted success, manager of Drury Lane Theater. The relation
between him and his old preceptor was of a very singular kind.
They repelled each other strongly, and yet attracted each other
strongly. Nature had made them of very different clay; and

---

[1] Commander of the pretorian guard under the Roman Emperor Tiberius.
He was put to death (A.D. 31) for his infamous crimes.

[2] The famous Carthaginian general (247–183 B.C.) who crossed the Alps,
and invaded Italy.

[3] Charles XII. of Sweden (1697–1718), famous for his military genius.
Johnson portrays Charles's ambition in lines 191–222 of the poem, ending : —

> " He left the name, at which the world grew pale,
> To point a moral, or adorn a tale."

[4] " There mark what ills the scholar's life assail, —
> Toil, envy, want, the garret [Patron], and the jail."
>
> *Vanity of Human Wishes,* lines 159, 160.

[5] Greatest of Greek orators (died, 322 B.C.).

[6] Greatest of Roman orators (106–43 B.C.)

circumstances had fully brought out the natural peculiarities of
both. Sudden prosperity had turned Garrick's head. Continued
adversity had soured Johnson's temper. Johnson saw, with more
envy than became so great a man, the villa, the plate, the china,
the Brussels carpet, which the little mimic had got by repeating,
with grimaces and gesticulations, what wiser men had written;
and the exquisitely sensitive vanity of Garrick was galled by the
thought, that, while all the rest of the world was applauding him,
he could obtain from one morose cynic,[1] whose opinion it was
impossible to despise, scarcely any compliment not acidulated
with scorn.   Yet the two Lichfield men had so many early recollections in common, and sympathized with each other on so
many points on which they sympathized with nobody else in the
vast population of the capital, that though the master was often
provoked by the monkeylike impertinence of the pupil, and the
pupil by the bearish rudeness of the master, they remained friends
till they were parted by death.   Garrick now brought "Irene"
out, with alterations sufficient to displease the author, yet not
sufficient to make the piece pleasing to the audience.   The public, however, listened, with little emotion, but with much civility,
to five acts of monotonous declamation.   After nine representa-
tions, the play was withdrawn. It is, indeed, altogether unsuited
to the stage, and, even when perused in the closet, will be found
hardly worthy of the author.   He had not the slightest notion of
what blank verse should be.   A change in the last syllable of
every other line would make the versification of the "Vanity of
Human Wishes" closely resemble the versification of "Irene."
The poet, however, cleared, by his benefit nights[2] and by the
sale of the copyright of his tragedy, about three hundred pounds,
then a great sum in his estimation.

[1] This name, now applied to a snappish or sneering faultfinder, was originally given to a Greek sect of philosophers noted for their coarse manners
and surly disposition.

[2] The profits of every third performance of a play fell to the author as his
benefit.

About a year after the representation of " Irene," he began to publish a series of short essays on morals, manners, and literature. This species of composition had been brought into fashion by the success of the " Tatler " and by the still more brilliant success of the " Spectator." [1]   A crowd of small writers had vainly attempted to rival Addison.[2]   The " Lay Monastery," the " Censor," the " Freethinker," the " Plain Dealer," the " Champion," and other works of the same kind, had had their short day.   None of them had obtained a permanent place in our literature; and they are now to be found only in the libraries of the curious.   At length Johnson undertook the adventure in which so many aspirants had failed.   In the thirty-sixth year after the appearance of the last number of the " Spectator," appeared the first number of the " Rambler."   From March, 1750, to March, 1752, this paper continued to come out every Tuesday and Saturday.

From the first, the " Rambler " was enthusiastically admired by a few eminent men.   Richardson,[3] when only five numbers had appeared, pronounced it equal, if not superior, to the " Spectator." Young[4] and Hartley[5] expressed their approbation not less warmly. Bubb Dodington,[6] among whose many faults indifference to the claims of genius and learning cannot be reckoned, solicited the acquaintance of the writer.   In consequence, probably, of the good offices of Dodington, who was then the confidential adviser

[1] The Tatler (1709) and the Spectator (1711) were projected by Richard Steele (1671–1729).   They mark the beginning of the periodical essay.

[2] Joseph Addison (1672–1719), essayist, famous for the ease, grace, and delicate humor of his style.   Associated with Steele, he made the fame of the Spectator.   In his day he also made a figure as a poet (Blenheim) and as a dramatist (Cato).

[3] Samuel Richardson (1689–1761), author of Pamela, Clarissa Harlowe, and Sir Charles Grandison.

[4] Dr. Edward Young (1681–1765), author of Night Thoughts.

[5] David Hartley (1705–57), philosopher; author of Observations on Man.

[6] Lord Melcombe (1691–1762), courtier and politician; satirized as Bubo by Pope.   His Diary gives an insight into the Whig intrigues of the time.

of Prince Frederick, two of his Royal Highness's gentlemen carried a gracious message to the printing office, and ordered seven copies for Leicester House.[1] But these overtures seem to have been very coldly received. Johnson had had enough of the patronage of the great to last him all his life, and was not disposed to haunt any other door as he had haunted the door of Chesterfield.

By the public the " Rambler " was at first very coldly received. Though the price of a number was only twopence, the sale did not amount to five hundred. The profits were therefore very small. But as soon as the flying leaves were collected and reprinted, they became popular. The author lived to see thirteen thousand copies spread over England alone. Separate editions were published for the Scotch and Irish markets. A large party pronounced the style perfect, so absolutely perfect, that in some essays it would be impossible for the writer himself to alter a single word for the better. Another party, not less numerous, vehemently accused him of having corrupted the purity of the English tongue. The best critics admitted that his diction was too monotonous, too obviously artificial, and now and then turgid even to absurdity. But they did justice to the acuteness of his observations on morals and manners, to the constant precision and frequent brilliancy of his language, to the weighty and magnificent eloquence of many serious passages, and to the solemn yet pleasing humor of some of the lighter papers. On the question of precedence between Addison and Johnson,—a question which, seventy years ago, was much disputed,—posterity has pronounced a decision from which there is no appeal. Sir Roger, his chaplain and his butler, Will Wimble and Will Honeycomb, the " Vision of Mirza," the " Journal of the Retired Citizen," the " Everlasting Club," the " Dunmow Flitch," the " Loves of Hilpah and Shalum," the " Visit to the Exchange," and the " Visit to the

---

[1] Frederick, Prince of Wales (1707-51), son of George II., resided at Leicester House from 1737 until his death. He quarreled with his father, and became a member " of the opposition," against Walpole and the King.

Abbey," are known to everybody.[1] But many men and women, even of highly cultivated minds, are unacquainted with Squire Bluster and Mrs. Busy, Quisquilius and Venustulus, the " Allegory of Wit and Learning," the " Chronicle of the Revolutions of a Garret," and the sad fate of Aningait and Ajut.[2]

The last " Rambler " was written in a sad and gloomy hour. Mrs. Johnson had been given over by the physicians. Three days later she died. She left her husband almost broken-hearted. Many people had been surprised to see a man of his genius and learning stooping to every drudgery, and denying himself almost every comfort, for the purpose of supplying a silly, affected old woman with superfluities, which she accepted with but little gratitude. But all his affection had been concentrated on her. He had neither brother nor sister, neither son nor daughter. To him she was beautiful as the Gunnings,[3] and witty as Lady Mary.[4] Her opinion of his writings was more important to him than the voice of the pit of Drury Lane Theater,[5] or the judgment of the " Monthly Review." The chief support which had sustained him through the most arduous labor of his life was the hope that she would enjoy the fame and the profit which he anticipated from his Dictionary. She was gone ; and in that vast labyrinth of streets, peopled by eight hundred thousand human beings, he was alone. Yet it was necessary for him to set himself, as he expressed it, doggedly to work. After three more laborious years, the Dictionary was at length complete.

[1] See Spectator : No. 159 (Mirza) ; No. 317 (Journal) ; No. 72 (Everlasting Club) ; Nos. 584, 585 (Hilpa) ; No. 69 (Royal Exchange). Sir Roger and the other familiar characters and chapters of the De Coverley Papers need no special reference.

[2] See Rambler, Nos. 142, 138, 82, 22, 161, and 186 respectively.

[3] The two Gunning sisters, — the Duchess of Hamilton and the Countess of Coventry, — famous beauties in the middle of the eighteenth century (see Dictionary of National Biography).

[4] Lady Mary Wortley Montagu (1689–1762), distinguished for her literary attainments and her Letters to Pope, Addison, and other eminent men.

[5] See Note 2, p. 30.

It had been generally supposed that this great work would be dedicated to the eloquent and accomplished nobleman to whom the Prospectus had been addressed. He well knew the value of such a compliment; and therefore, when the day of publication drew near, he exerted himself to soothe, by a show of zealous and at the same time of delicate and judicious kindness, the pride which he had so cruelly wounded. Since the "Ramblers" had ceased to appear, the town had been entertained by a journal called the "World," to which many men of high rank and fashion contributed.[1] In two successive numbers of the "World" the Dictionary was, to use the modern phrase, puffed with wonderful skill. The writings of Johnson were warmly praised. It was proposed that he should be invested with the authority of a dictator, nay, of a pope, over our language, and that his decisions about the meaning and the spelling of words should be received as final. His two folios, it was said, would of course be bought by everybody who could afford to buy them. It was soon known that these papers were written by Chesterfield. But the just resentment of Johnson was not to be so appeased. In a letter[2] written with singular energy and dignity of thought and language, he repelled the tardy advances of his patron. The Dictionary came forth without a dedication. In the Preface the author truly declared that he owed nothing to the great, and described the difficulties with which he had been left to struggle so forcibly and pathetically, that the ablest and most malevolent of all the enemies of his fame, Horne Tooke,[3] never could read that passage without tears.

The public, on this occasion, did Johnson full justice, and something more than justice. The best lexicographer may well

---

[1] Among the contributors were Chesterfield and Horace ("Horry") Walpole (1717–97). The editor was Edward Moore.

[2] See Introduction.

[3] The assumed name of John Horne (1736–1812), politician and philologist; author of Diversions of Purley. He was tried for high treason, but acquitted (1794). He criticised Johnson's etymologies.

be content if his productions are received by the world with cold esteem. But Johnson's Dictionary was hailed with an enthusiasm such as no similar work has ever excited. It was, indeed, the first dictionary which could be read with pleasure. The definitions[1] show so much acuteness of thought and command of language, and the passages quoted from poets, divines, and philosophers, are so skillfully selected, that a leisure hour may always be very agreeably spent in turning over the pages. The faults of the book resolve themselves, for the most part, into one great fault. Johnson was a wretched etymologist. He knew little or nothing of any Teutonic language except English, which, indeed, as he wrote it, was scarcely a Teutonic language; and thus he was absolutely at the mercy of Junius[2] and Skinner.[3]

The Dictionary, though it raised Johnson's fame, added nothing to his pecuniary means. The fifteen hundred guineas which the booksellers had agreed to pay him had been advanced and spent before the last sheets issued from the press. It is painful to relate, that, twice in the course of the year which followed the publication of this great work, he was arrested and carried to sponginghouses,[4] and that he was twice indebted for his liberty to his excellent friend Richardson.[5] It was still necessary for the man who had been formally saluted by the highest authority as dictator of the English language, to supply his wants by constant toil. He abridged his Dictionary. He proposed to bring out an edition of Shakespeare by subscription; and many subscribers sent in their names, and laid down their money; but he soon found the

---

1 Many of the definitions were inserted in a spirit of humor and mischief. "Lexicographer" he defined as "a harmless drudge;" and "oats" as "a grain which in England is generally given to horses, but in Scotland supports the people."

2 Francis Junius (1589–1677), student of the Teutonic languages.

3 Dr. Stephen Skinner (1623–67), lexicographer.

4 "A house to which debtors are taken before commitment to prison, where the bailiffs sponge upon them, or riot at their cost."—JOHNSON: *Dictionary.*

5 See Note 3, p. 41.

task so little to his taste that he turned to more attractive employ-
ments. He contributed many papers to a new monthly journal,
which was called the "Literary Magazine." Few of these papers
have much interest; but among them was the very best thing that
he ever wrote, a masterpiece both of reasoning and of satirical
pleasantry, the review of Jenyns's[1] "Inquiry into the Nature and
Origin of Evil."

In the spring of 1758 Johnson put forth the first of a series of
essays entitled the "Idler." During two years these essays continued to appear weekly. They were eagerly read, widely circu-
lated, and, indeed, impudently pirated while they were still in the
original form, and had a large sale when collected into volumes.
The "Idler" may be described as a second part of the "Rambler," somewhat livelier and somewhat weaker than the first
part.

While Johnson was busied with his "Idlers," his mother, who
had accomplished her ninetieth year, died at Lichfield. It was
long since he had seen her; but he had not failed to contribute
largely, out of his small means, to her comfort. In order to
defray the charges of her funeral, and to pay some debts which
she had left, he wrote a little book in a single week, and sent off
the sheets to the press without reading them over. A hundred
pounds were paid him for the copyright; and the purchasers had
great cause to be pleased with their bargain, for the book was
"Rasselas."[2]

The success of "Rasselas" was great, though such ladies as
Miss Lydia Languish[3] must have been grievously disappointed
when they found that the new volume from the circulating library
was little more than a dissertation on the author's favorite theme,
the vanity of human wishes; that the Prince of Abyssinia was
without a mistress, and the princess without a lover; and that the
story set the hero and the heroine down exactly where it had taken

[1] Soame Jenyns (1704–87), miscellaneous writer.
[2] Rasselas; or, the Prince of Abyssinia, appeared in 1759.
[3] A sentimental character in Sheridan's Rivals.

them up. The style was the subject of much eager controversy. The " Monthly Review " and the " Critical Review " took different sides. Many readers pronounced the writer a pompous pedant, who would never use a word of two syllables where it was possible to use a word of six, and who could not make a waiting woman relate her adventures without balancing every noun with another noun, and every epithet with another epithet. Another party, not less zealous, cited with delight numerous passages in which weighty meaning was expressed with accuracy, and illustrated with splendor. And both the censure and the praise were merited.

About the plan of " Rasselas " little was said by the critics ; and yet the faults of the plan might seem to invite severe criticism. Johnson has frequently blamed Shakespeare for neglecting the proprieties of time and place, and for ascribing to one age or nation the manners and opinions of another. Yet Shakespeare has not sinned in this way more grievously than Johnson. Rasselas and Imlac, Nekayah and Pekuah,[1] are evidently meant to be Abyssinians of the eighteenth century ; for the Europe which Imlac describes is the Europe of the eighteenth century ; and the inmates of the Happy Valley talk familiarly of that law of gravitation which Newton [2] discovered, and which was not fully received, even at Cambridge,[3] till the eighteenth century. What a real company of Abyssinians would have been may be learned from Bruce's [4] "Travels." But Johnson, not content with turning filthy savages ignorant of their letters, and gorged with raw steaks cut from living cows, into philosophers as eloquent and enlightened as himself or his friend Burke,[5] and into ladies as highly

---

[1] Imlac the poet, Nekayah the princess, and Pekuah the favorite companion of the princess, are all characters in Rasselas.

[2] Sir Isaac Newton (1642–1727), greatest of English mathematicians and astronomers.

[3] See Note 4, p. 23.

[4] James Bruce (1730–94), celebrated African traveler.

[5] Edmund Burke (1729–97), orator and statesman ; friend of America.

accomplished as Mrs. Lennox [1] or Mrs. Sheridan,[2] transferred the whole domestic system of England to Egypt. Into a land of harems, a land of polygamy, a land where women are married without ever being seen, he introduced the flirtations and jealousies of our ballrooms. In a land where there is boundless liberty of divorce, wedlock is described as the indissoluble compact. " A youth and maiden meeting by chance, or brought together by artifice, exchange glances, reciprocate civilities, go home and dream of each other. Such," says Rasselas, " is the common process of marriage." Such it may have been, and may still be, in London, but assuredly not at Cairo. A writer who was guilty of such improprieties had little right to blame the poet who made Hector quote Aristotle,[3] and represented Julio Romano [4] as flourishing in the days of the oracle of Delphi.

By such exertions as have been described, Johnson supported himself till the year 1762. In that year a great change in his circumstances took place. He had from a child been an enemy of the reigning dynasty. [/] His Jacobite prejudices had been exhibited with little disguise both in his works and in his conversation. Even in his massy and elaborate Dictionary, he had, with a strange want of taste and judgment, inserted bitter and contumelious reflections on the Whig party. The excise, which was a favorite resource of Whig financiers, he had designated as a hateful tax. He had railed against the commissioners of excise in language so coarse that they had seriously thought of prosecuting him. He had with difficulty been prevented from holding

---

[1] Mrs. Charlotte Ramsay Lennox (1720–1804), author of Female Quixote, and Life of Harriet Stuart.

[2] Mrs. Frances Sheridan (1724–66), mother of the dramatist; author of Memoirs of Miss Sidney Biddulph.

[3] Shakespeare (see Troilus and Cressida, act ii. sc. 2). Hector was the Trojan hero in the traditional siege of Troy; and Aristotle (died, 322 B.C.), the most famous of the Greek philosophers.

[4] See Winter's Tale, act v. sc. 2. Giulio Romano (1492–1546) was a celebrated Italian painter. The oracle of Apollo at Delphi (Phocis, Greece) was famous in antiquity.

up the lord privy seal [1] by name as an example of the meaning
of the word "renegade." A pension he had defined as pay given
to a state hireling to betray his country ; a pensioner, as a slave
of state hired by a stipend to obey a master. It seemed unlikely
that the author of these definitions would himself be pensioned.
But that was a time of wonders. George III. had ascended the
throne,[2] and had, in the course of a few months, disgusted many
of the old friends, and conciliated many of the old enemies, of his
house. The city was becoming mutinous. Oxford was becoming loyal. Cavendishes and Bentincks were murmuring. Somersets and Wyndhams [3] were hastening to kiss hands. The head
of the treasury was now Lord Bute,[4] who was a Tory, and could
have no objection to Johnson's Toryism. Bute wished to be
thought a patron of men of letters ; and Johnson was one of the
most eminent and one of the most needy men of letters in Europe.
A pension of three hundred a year was graciously offered, and
with very little hesitation accepted.

This event produced a change in Johnson's whole way of life.
For the first time since his boyhood, he no longer felt the daily
goad urging him to the daily toil. He was at liberty, after thirty
years of anxiety and drudgery, to indulge his constitutional indolence, to lie in bed till two in the afternoon, and to sit up talking
till four in the morning, without fearing either the printer's devil
or the sheriff's officer. •

One laborious task, indeed, he had bound himself to perform.

---

[1] The custodian of the privy seal, which is affixed to minor documents, and
which is also used in connection with the great seal of the government (the
chief emblem of sovereignty). Johnson added to the definition of " renegade "
the words, " Sometimes we say a Gower ;" but they were struck out by the
printer.

[2] 1760.

[3] The Cavendishes and Bentincks were representative Whig, and the
Somersets and Wyndhams representative Tory families. On the death of
Queen Anne (1714), Sir William Wyndham built up a Jacobite party.

[4] Earl of Bute (1713–92), a court favorite, and puppet of George III. He
became premier in 1762.

4

He had received large subscriptions for his promised edition of Shakespeare; he had lived on those subscriptions during some years; and he could not, without disgrace, omit to perform his part of the contract. His friends repeatedly exhorted him to make an effort; and he repeatedly resolved to do so. But, notwithstanding their exhortations and his resolutions, month followed month, year followed year, and nothing was done. He prayed fervently against his idleness; he determined, as often as he received the sacrament, that he would no longer doze away and trifle away his time; but the spell under which he lay resisted prayer and sacrament. His private notes at this time are made up of self-reproaches. "My indolence," he wrote on Easter Eve in 1764, "has sunk into grosser sluggishness. A kind of strange oblivion has overspread me, so that I know not what has become of the last year." Easter, 1765, came, and found him still in the same state. "My time," he wrote, "has been unprofitably spent, and seems as a dream that has left nothing behind. My memory grows confused, and I know not how the days pass over me." Happily for his honor, the charm which held him captive was at length broken by no gentle or friendly hand. He had been weak enough to pay serious attention to a story about a ghost which haunted a house in Cock Lane,[1] and had actually gone himself, with some of his friends, at one in the morning, to St. John's Church, Clerkenwell,[2] in the hope of receiving a communication from the perturbed spirit. But the spirit, though adjured with all solemnity, remained obstinately silent; and it soon appeared that a naughty girl of eleven had been amusing herself by making fools of so many philosophers. Churchill,[3] who, con-

---

[1] This story was woven about the adventures of a young girl in Cock Lane, London (1762), who pretended to be in communication with the world of spirits. As a matter of fact, Johnson assisted in detecting the imposture.

[2] A northern district of London.

[3] Charles Churchill (1731–64), poet and wit. He has all the bitterness of Pope.

fident in his powers, drunk with popularity, and burning with party spirit, was looking for some man of established fame and Tory politics to insult, celebrated the Cock Lane ghost in three cantos, nicknamed Johnson Pomposo, asked where the book was which had been so long promised and so liberally paid for, and directly accused the great moralist of cheating. This terrible word proved effectual; and in October, 1765, appeared, after a delay of nine years, the new edition of Shakespeare.

This publication saved Johnson's character for honesty, but added nothing to the fame of his abilities and learning. The preface, though it contains some good passages, is not in his best manner. The most valuable notes are those in which he had an opportunity of showing how attentively he had, during many years, observed human life and human nature. The best specimen is the note on the character of Polonius.[1] Nothing so good is to be found even in Wilhelm Meister's [2] admirable examination of Hamlet. But here praise must end. It would be difficult to name a more slovenly, a more worthless, edition of any great classic. The reader may turn over play after play without finding one happy conjectural emendation, or one ingenious and satisfactory explanation of a passage which had baffled preceding commentators. Johnson had, in his Prospectus, told the world that he was peculiarly fitted for the task which he had undertaken, because he had, as a lexicographer, been under the necessity of taking a wider view of the English language than any of his predecessors. That his knowledge of our literature was extensive, is indisputable. But, unfortunately, he had altogether neglected that very part of our literature with which it is especially desirable that an editor of Shakespeare should be conversant. It is dangerous to assert a negative. Yet little will be risked by the assertion, that in the two folio volumes of the " English Dictionary " there is not a single passage quoted from any dramatist of

---

[1] The royal chamberlain in Hamlet; the father of Ophelia.

[2] Wilhelm Meister's Lehrjahre, by Johann Wolfgang von Goethe (1749–1832), whose name is the greatest in German literature (see Bk. IV. xiii.).

the Elizabethan age,[1] except Shakespeare and Ben.[2] Even from Ben the quotations are few. Johnson might easily, in a few months, have made himself well acquainted with every old play that was extant. But it never seems to have occurred to him that this was a necessary preparation for the work which he had undertaken. He would doubtless have admitted that it would be the height of absurdity in a man who was not familiar with the works of Æschylus and Euripides to publish an edition of Sophocles.[3] Yet he ventured to publish an edition of Shakespeare without having ever in his life, as far as can be discovered, read a single scene of Massinger,[4] Ford, Dekker, Webster, Marlowe, Beaumont, or Fletcher. His detractors were noisy and scurrilous. Those who most loved and honored him had little to say in praise of the manner in which he had discharged the duty of a commentator. He had, however, acquitted himself of a debt which had long lain heavy on his conscience, and he sank back into the repose from which the sting of satire had roused him. He long continued to live upon the fame which he had already won. He was honored by the University of Oxford with a doc-

[1] This great age of English poetry ended, strictly speaking, with the death of Queen Elizabeth, in 1603; but the name is extended to cover the period up to the Restoration (1660).

[2] "Rare Ben Jonson" (1573-1637), the most famous of the dramatists contemporary with Shakespeare.

[3] Æschylus (died, 456 B.C.), Sophocles (died, 406 B.C.), and Euripides (died, 406 B.C.) were the three great tragic poets of Greece.

[4] Here follows a list of the most famous Elizabethan and Stuart dramatists : Philip Massinger (1584-1640), author of A New Way to Pay Old Debts ; John Ford (1586 to about 1639), author of Broken Heart and Perkin Warbeck ; Thomas Dekker (about 1570 to about 1637); John Webster, a dramatist of "intense and somber genius," who wrote Duchess of Malfi and Vittoria Corombona; Christopher Marlowe (1564-93), an early contemporary of Shakespeare, and author of Tamburlaine (in which he popularized blank verse), Edward II., and Dr. Faustus ; and Francis Beaumont (1584-1616) and his collaborator John Fletcher (1579-1625). Beaumont and Fletcher, the most important of the Stuart dramatists, produced in the reign of James I. fifty-three plays, only thirteen being joint productions.

tor's degree, by the Royal Academy [1] with a professorship, and by the King with an interview, in which his Majesty most graciously expressed a hope that so excellent a writer would not cease to write. In the interval, however, between 1765 and 1775, Johnson published only two or three political tracts, the longest of which he could have produced in forty-eight hours, if he had worked as he worked on the "Life of Savage" and on "Rasselas."

But, though his pen was now idle, his tongue was active. The influence exercised by his conversation, directly upon those with whom he lived, and indirectly on the whole literary world, was altogether without a parallel. His colloquial talents were, indeed, of the highest order. He had strong sense, quick discernment, wit, humor, immense knowledge of literature and of life, and an infinite store of curious anecdotes. As respected style, he spoke far better than he wrote. Every sentence which dropped from his lips was as correct in structure as the most nicely balanced period of the "Rambler." But in his talk there were no pompous triads, and little more than a fair proportion of words in "osity" and "ation." All was simplicity, ease, and vigor. He uttered his short, weighty, and pointed sentences with a power of voice and a justness and energy of emphasis of which the effect was rather increased than diminished by the rollings of his huge form, and by the asthmatic gaspings and puffings in which the peals of his eloquence generally ended. Nor did the laziness which made him unwilling to sit down to his desk prevent him from giving instruction or entertainment orally. To discuss questions of taste, of learning, of casuistry, in language so exact and so forcible that it might have been printed without the alteration of a word, was to him no exertion, but a pleasure. He loved, as he said, to fold his legs and have his talk out. He was ready to bestow the overflowings of his full mind on anybody who would start a subject.—on a fellow-passenger in a stagecoach, or

[1] The Royal Academy of Arts, instituted under the patronage of George III., Sir Joshua Reynolds being the first president. Its first meeting was held in 1768.

on the person who sat at the same table with him in an eating house. But his conversation was nowhere so brilliant and striking as when he was surrounded by a few friends, whose abilities and knowledge enabled them, as he once expressed it, to send him back every ball that he threw. Some of these, in 1764, formed themselves into a club,[1] which gradually became a formidable power in the commonwealth of letters. The verdicts pronounced by this conclave on new books were speedily known over all London, and were sufficient to sell off a whole edition in a day, or to condemn the sheets to the service of the trunk maker and the pastry cook. Nor shall we think this strange when we consider what great and various talents and acquirements met in the little fraternity. Goldsmith[2] was the representative of poetry and light literature; Reynolds,[3] of the arts; Burke, of political eloquence and political philosophy. There, too, were Gibbon,[4] the greatest historian, and Jones,[5] the greatest linguist, of the age. Garrick brought to the meetings his inexhaustible pleasantry, his incomparable mimicry, and his consummate knowledge of stage effect. Among the most constant attendants were two high-born and high-bred gentlemen, closely bound together by friendship, but of widely different characters and habits,—Bennet Langton,[6] distinguished by his skill in Greek literature, by the orthodoxy of his opinions, and by the sanctity of his life; and Topham Beauclerk,[7]

[1] The Literary Club, which met at the Turk's Head, Soho.

[2] Oliver Goldsmith (1728–74), poet, novelist, and dramatist. His Vicar of Wakefield is a famous classic.

[3] Sir Joshua Reynolds (1723–92), one of the most famous of English portrait painters.

[4] Edward Gibbon (1737–94), author of Decline and Fall of the Roman Empire.

[5] Sir William Jones (1746–94), scholar, Oriental linguist, and jurist.

[6] A scholar of amiable character (1737–1801), greatly beloved by Johnson. He succeeded Johnson as professor of ancient literature at the Royal Academy.

[7] Son of Lord Sidney Beauclerk, and grandson of the Duke of St. Albans (1739–80); "commended to Johnson by a likeness to Charles II., from whom he was descended."

renowned for his amours, his knowledge of the gay world, his fastidious taste, and his sarcastic wit. To predominate over such a society was not easy. Yet even over such a society John-son predominated. Burke might, indeed, have disputed the su-premacy to which others were under the necessity of submitting. But Burke, though not generally a very patient listener, was con-tent to take the second part when Johnson was present; and the club itself, consisting of so many eminent men, is to this day popularly designated as Johnson's Club.

Among the members of this celebrated body was one to whom it has owed the greater part of its celebrity, yet who was regarded with little respect by his brethren, and had not without difficulty obtained a seat among them. This was James Boswell,[1] a young Scotch lawyer, heir to an honorable name and a fair estate. That he was a coxcomb and a bore, weak, vain, pushing, curious, garrulous, was obvious to all who were acquainted with him. That he could not reason, that he had no wit, no humor, no elo-quence, is apparent from his writings. And yet his writings are read beyond the Mississippi and under the Southern Cross,[2] and are likely to be read as long as the English exists, either as a liv-ing or as a dead language. Nature had made him a slave and an idolater. His mind resembled those creepers which the botanists call parasites, and which can subsist only by clinging round the stems, and imbibing the juices, of stronger plants. He must have fastened himself on somebody. He might have fastened himself on Wilkes,[3] and have become the fiercest patriot in the Bill of

[1] See Introduction.

[2] A small brilliant constellation of the southern hemisphere, so called from the arrangement of its four principal stars.

[3] John Wilkes (1727–97), editor of the *North Briton*; several times ex-pelled from Parliament, and reëlected from Middlesex. Though a notorious demagogue, he was nevertheless among the first to establish the right of the press to discuss parliamentary proceedings and public affairs, and he became for a time the popular idol. The Society for the Support of the Bill of Rights (1769) was founded to help Wilkes in his constitutional struggle with Parliament.

Rights Society. He might have fastened himself on Whitefield,[1] and have become the loudest field preacher among the Calvinistic Methodists. In a happy hour he fastened himself on Johnson. The pair might seem ill-matched. For Johnson had early been prejudiced against Boswell's country. To a man of Johnson's strong understanding and irritable temper, the silly egotism and adulation of Boswell must have been as teasing as the constant buzz of a fly. Johnson hated to be questioned; and Boswell was eternally catechising him on all kinds of subjects, and sometimes propounded such questions as, "What would you do, sir, if you were locked up in a tower with a baby?" Johnson was a water drinker, and Boswell was a winebibber, and, indeed, little better than an habitual sot. It was impossible that there should be perfect harmony between two such companions. Indeed, the great man was sometimes provoked into fits of passion, in which he said things which the small man, during a few hours, seriously resented. Every quarrel, however, was soon made up. During twenty years, the disciple continued to worship the master: the master continued to scold the disciple, to sneer at him, and to love him. The two friends ordinarily resided at a great distance from each other. Boswell practiced in the Parliament House of Edinburgh, and could pay only occasional visits to London. During those visits, his chief business was to watch Johnson, to discover all Johnson's habits, to turn the conversation to subjects about which Johnson was likely to say something remarkable, and to fill quarto notebooks with minutes of what Johnson had said. In this way were gathered the materials out of which was afterwards constructed the most interesting biographical work[2] in the world.

Soon after the club began to exist, Johnson formed a connec-

---

[1] George Whitefield (1714–70), the great preacher of the Methodist revival. Wesley, the head of the Methodists, broke with Whitefield, who had "plunged into an extravagant Calvinism," and who became the founder of the sect called "Calvinistic Methodists." Whitefield, as a follower of John Calvin (1509–64), accepted the doctrine of predestination.

[2] See Dr. Birkbeck Hill's edition (1887, 6 vols.).

tion less important, indeed. to his fame, but much more important to his happiness, than his connection with Boswell. Henry
Thrale, one of the most opulent brewers in the kingdom, a man
of sound and cultivated understanding, rigid principles, and liberal
spirit, was married to one of those clever, kind-hearted, engaging,
vain, pert young women who are perpetually doing or saying what
is not exactly right. but who, do or say what they may, are always
agreeable.[1] In 1765 the Thrales became acquainted with Johnson, and the acquaintance ripened fast into friendship. They
were astonished and delighted by the brilliancy of his conversation. They were flattered by finding that a man so widely celebrated preferred their house to any other in London. Even the
peculiarities which seemed to unfit him for civilized society—his
gesticulations, his rollings, his puffings, his mutterings, the strange
way in which he put on his clothes, the ravenous eagerness with
which he devoured his dinner, his fits of melancholy, his fits of
anger, his frequent rudeness, his occasional ferocity—increased
the interest which his new associates took in him. 'For these
things were the cruel marks left behind by a life which had been
one long conflict with disease and with adversity.' In a vulgar
hack writer, such oddities would have excited only disgust; but
in a man of genius, learning. and virtue, their effect was to add
pity to admiration and esteem. Johnson soon had an apartment
at the brewery in Southwark, and a still more pleasant apartment at the villa of his friends on Streatham Common. A large
part of every year he passed in those abodes,—abodes which must
have seemed magnificent and luxurious indeed, when compared
with the dens in which he had generally been lodged. But his
chief pleasures were derived from what the astronomer of his
Abyssinian tale called "the endearing elegance of female friendship." Mrs. Thrale rallied him, soothed him, coaxed him, and,

---

[1] In 1763, Hester Lynch Salisbury (1741-1821) married Henry Thrale,
member of Parliament for Southwark. After Thrale's death (1781), she
married Gabriel Piozzi, an Italian music teacher. Her Anecdotes of Johnson
appeared in 1786.

if she sometimes provoked him by her flippancy, made ample amends by listening to his reproofs with angelic sweetness of temper. When he was diseased in body and in mind, she was the most tender of nurses. No comfort that wealth could purchase, no contrivance that womanly ingenuity, set to work by womanly compassion, could devise, was wanting to his sick room. He requited her kindness by an affection pure as the affection of a father, yet delicately tinged with a gallantry which, though awkward, must have been more flattering than the attentions of a crowd of the fools who gloried in the names, now obsolete, of buck and maccaroni.[1] It should seem that a full half of Johnson's life, during about sixteen years, was passed under the roof of the Thrales. He accompanied the family sometimes to Bath,[2] and sometimes to Brighton,[3] once to Wales, and once to Paris.[4] But he had at the same time a house in one of the narrow and gloomy courts[5] on the north of Fleet Street. In the garrets was his library, a large and miscellaneous collection of books, falling to pieces, and begrimed with dust. On a lower floor he sometimes, but very rarely, regaled a friend with a plain dinner,—a veal pie, or a leg of lamb and spinach, and a rice pudding. Nor was the dwelling uninhabited during his long absences. It was the home of the most extraordinary assemblage of inmates that ever was brought together. At the head of the establishment, Johnson had placed an old lady named Williams, whose chief recommendations were her blindness and her poverty. But, in spite of her murmurs and reproaches, he gave an asylum to another lady who was as poor as herself, Mrs. Desmoulins, whose family he had known many years before in Staffordshire. Room

1 Fop or dandy (see Century Dictionary).

2 One of the leading watering places of England; especially noted in the eighteenth century, when Beau Nash was master of ceremonies, or " King of Bath " (see Goldsmith's Life of Richard Nash).

3 On the English Channel; now the leading seaside resort in Great Britain.   4 In 1775.

5 Bolt Court, where Johnson lived from 1776 up to the time of his death.

was found for the daughter of Mrs. Desmoulins, and for another
destitute damsel, who was generally addressed as Miss Carmichael,
but whom her generous host called Polly. An old quack doctor
named Levett, who bled and dosed coal heavers and hackney
coachmen, and received for fees crusts of bread, bits of bacon,
glasses of gin, and sometimes a little copper, completed this
strange menagerie. All these poor creatures were at constant
war with each other and with Johnson's negro servant Frank.
Sometimes, indeed, they transferred their hostilities from the servant to the master, complained that a better table was not kept
for them, and railed or maundered till their benefactor was glad
to make his escape to Streatham, or to the Mitre Tavern.[1] And
yet he, who was generally the haughtiest and most irritable of
mankind, who was but too prompt to resent anything which
looked like a slight on the part of a purse-proud bookseller, or of
a noble and powerful patron, bore patiently from mendicants,
who but for his bounty must have gone to the workhouse, in-
sults more provoking than those for which he had knocked down
Osborne,[2] and bidden defiance to Chesterfield. Year after year
Mrs. Williams and Mrs. Desmoulins, Polly and Levett, continued
to torment him and to live upon him.

The course of life which has been described was interrupted in
Johnson's sixty-fourth year by an important event. He had
early read an account of the Hebrides, and had been much in-
terested by learning that there was so near him a land peopled
by a race which was still as rude and simple as in the middle
ages.[3] A wish to become intimately acquainted with a state of

1 The celebrated tavern in Fleet Street, London, where Boswell and
Johnson frequently met, and where they planned the famous tour to the
Hebrides.

2 Thomas Osborne, a bookseller in Gray's Inn, satirized in the Dunciad
(Book II. 167). "He was impertinent to me," said Johnson, "and I beat
him. But it was not in his shop; it was in my own chamber."

3 The middle ages include the interval from the close of the fourth
century to the middle of the fifteenth century, when the modern era
began.

society so utterly unlike all that he had ever seen, frequently
crossed his mind. But it is not probable that his curiosity would
have overcome his habitual sluggishness and his love of the
smoke, the mud, and the cries of London, had not Boswell im-
portuned him to attempt the adventure, and offered to be his
squire.[1] At length, in August, 1773, Johnson crossed the High-
land line, and plunged courageously into what was then considered, by most Englishmen, as a dreary and perilous wilderness.
After wandering about two months through the Celtic[2] region,
sometimes in rude boats which did not protect him from the rain,
and sometimes on small shaggy ponies which could hardly bear
his weight, he returned to his old haunts with a mind full of new
images and new theories. During the following year he employed
himself in recording his adventures. About the beginning of
1775, his "Journey to the Hebrides" was published, and was,
during some weeks, the chief subject of conversation in all circles
in which any attention was paid to literature. The book is still
read with pleasure. The narrative is entertaining; the specula-
tions, whether sound or unsound, are always ingenious; and the
style, though too stiff and pompous, is somewhat easier and more
graceful than that of his early writings. His prejudice against
the Scotch had at length become little more than matter of jest;
and whatever remained of the old feeling had been effectually
removed by the kind and respectful hospitality with which he had
been received in every part of Scotland. It was, of course, not
to be expected that an Oxonian Tory should praise the Presby-
terian polity and ritual, or that an eye accustomed to the hedge-
rows and parks of England should not be struck by the bareness
of Berwickshire and East Lothian.[3] But even in censure Johnson's tone is not unfriendly. The most enlightened Scotchmen,

---

[1] A term of chivalry for an attendant on a knight: used here in the general sense of "escort."

[2] The Highlanders of Scotland are called "Celtic" from the kinship of
their language to that of the Irish, the Welsh, and the Britons.

[3] Counties in southeastern Scotland.

with Lord Mansfield [1] at their head, were well pleased. But some foolish and ignorant Scotchmen were moved to anger by a little unpalatable truth which was mingled with much eulogy, and assailed him whom they chose to consider as the enemy of their country with libels much more dishonorable to their country than anything that he had ever said or written. They published paragraphs in the newspapers, articles in the magazines, sixpenny pamphlets, five-shilling books. One scribbler abused Johnson for being blear-eyed; another for being a pensioner; a third informed the world that one of the doctor's uncles had been convicted of felony in Scotland, and had found that there was in that country one tree capable of supporting the weight of an Englishman. Macpherson,[2] whose "Fingal" had been proved in the "Journey" to be an impudent forgery, threatened to take vengeance with a cane. The only effect of this threat was that Johnson reiterated the charge of forgery in the most contemptuous terms, and walked about, during some time, with a cudgel, which, if the impostor had not been too wise to encounter it, would assuredly have descended upon him, to borrow the sublime language of his own epic poem, "like a hammer on the red son of the furnace."

Of other assailants, Johnson took no notice whatever. He had early resolved never to be drawn into controversy; and he adhered to his resolution with a steadfastness which is the more extraordinary because he was, both intellectually and morally, of the stuff of which controversialists are made. In conversation, he was a singularly eager, acute, and pertinacious disputant. When at a loss for good reasons, he had recourse to sophistry; and when heated by altercation, he made unsparing use of sarcasm

---

[1] A celebrated jurist and statesman (1705-93).

[2] James Macpherson (1736-96) published some poems, including the epic Fingal, which professed to be translations of the works of Ossian, a Gaelic bard of the third century. The modern opinion is, that these "relics of ancient Celtic literature" were largely original with Macpherson. (See "Macpherson," in Dictionary of National Biography.)

and invective. But when he took his pen in his hand, his whole
character seemed to be changed.   A hundred bad writers misrep-
resented him and reviled him; but not one of the hundred could
boast of having been thought by him worthy of a refutation, or
even of a retort. The Kenricks, Campbells, MacNicols, and Hen-
dersons did their best to annoy him, in the hope that he would
give them importance by answering them.   But the reader will
in vain search his works for any allusion to Kenrick [1] or Campbell,[2] to MacNicol [3] or Henderson.[4]   One Scotchman, bent on
vindicating the fame of Scotch learning, defied him to the com-
bat in a detestable Latin hexameter—

> " Maxime, si tu vis, cupio contendere tecum." [5]

But Johnson took no notice of the challenge.   He had learned,
both from his own observation and from literary history, in which
he was deeply read, that the place of books in the public estimation is fixed, not by what is written about them, but by what
is written in them; and that an author whose works are likely
to live is very unwise if he stoops to wrangle with detractors
whose works are certain to die.   He always maintained that
fame was a shuttlecock, which could be kept up only by being
beaten back, as well as beaten forward, and which would soon
fall if there were only one battledoor.   No saying was oftener in
his mouth than that fine apothegm of Bentley,[6] that no man was
ever written down but by himself.

Unhappily, a few months after the appearance of the " Journey
to the Hebrides," Johnson did what none of his envious assailants

[1] Dr. William Kenrick (died, 1779), a vulgar satirist, who savagely attacked
Johnson's Shakespeare.

[2] Archibald Campbell, a Scotch purser in the navy, who satirized Johnson's style under the title of Lexiphanes.

[3] Rev. Donald MacNicol, who published a scurrilous volume on Johnson's
Journey to the Hebrides.

[4] Dr. Andrew Henderson, who likewise criticised Johnson's Journey.

[5] " I desire especially, if you wish, to contend with you."

[6] Richard Bentley (1662-1742), famous classical scholar.

could have done, and to a certain extent succeeded in writing himself down. The disputes between England and her American Colonies had reached a point at which no amicable adjustment was possible. Civil war was evidently impending; and the ministers seem to have thought that the eloquence of Johnson might with advantage be employed to inflame the nation against the opposition here, and against the rebels beyond the Atlantic. He had already written two or three tracts in defense of the foreign and domestic policy of the government; and those tracts, though hardly worthy of him, were much superior to the crowd of pamphlets which lay on the counters of Almon [1] and Stockdale. But his "Taxation no Tyranny" [2] was a pitiable failure. The very title was a silly phrase, which can have been recommended to his choice by nothing but a jingling alliteration which he ought to have despised. The arguments were such as boys use in debating societies. The pleasantry was as awkward as the gambols of a hippopotamus. Even Boswell was forced to own that in this unfortunate piece he could detect no trace of his master's powers. The general opinion was, that the strong faculties which had produced the Dictionary and the "Rambler" were beginning to feel the effect of time and of disease, and that the old man would best consult his credit by writing no more.

But this was a great mistake. Johnson had failed, not because his mind was less vigorous than when he wrote "Rasselas" in the evenings of a week, but because he had foolishly chosen, or suffered others to choose for him, a subject such as he would at no time have been competent to treat. He was in no sense a statesman. He never willingly read, or thought, or talked about, affairs of state. He loved biography, literary history, the history of manners; but political history was positively distasteful to him. The question at issue between the Colonies and the mother country was a question about which he had really nothing to say.

[1] John Almon (1737–1805), bookseller and journalist; friend of John Wilkes.

[2] Published in 1775.

He failed, therefore, as the greatest men must fail when they attempt to do that for which they are unfit; as Burke would have failed if Burke had tried to write comedies like those of Sheridan;[1] as Reynolds would have failed if Reynolds had tried to paint landscapes like those of Wilson.[2] Happily, Johnson soon had an opportunity of proving most signally that his failure was not to be ascribed to intellectual decay.

On Easter Eve, 1777, some persons, deputed by a meeting which consisted of forty of the first booksellers in London, called upon him. Though he had some scruples about doing business at that season, he received his visitors with much civility. They came to inform him that a new edition of the English poets, from Cowley downwards, was in contemplation, and to ask him to furnish short biographical prefaces. He readily undertook the task, a task for which he was preëminently qualified. His knowledge of the literary history of England since the Restoration was unrivaled. That knowledge he had derived partly from books, and partly from sources which had long been closed: from old Grub Street traditions; from the talk of forgotten poetasters and pamphleteers who had long been lying in parish vaults; from the recollections of such men as Gilbert Walmesley, who had conversed with the wits of Button;[3] Cibber,[4] who had mutilated the plays of two generations of dramatists; Orrery,[5] who had been admitted to the society of Swift;[6] and Savage,[7] who had rendered services of no very honorable kind to Pope. The biog-

---

[1] Richard Brinsley Butler Sheridan (1751–1816), noted dramatist and Whig politician; author of School for Scandal.

[2] Richard Wilson (1714–82), one of the original members of the Royal Academy.

[3] A famous coffeehouse in Queen Anne's time, frequented by Addison and his associates.

[4] Colley Cibber (1671–1757), actor and dramatist; poet laureate. Among the plays he altered were Richard III. and King Lear.

[5] John Boyle (1707–62), Earl of Orrery; author of a Life of Swift.

[6] Jonathan Swift (1667–1745), greatest of English satirists; author of Tale of a Tub and Gulliver's Travels.   [7] See Note 4, p. 35.

rapher, therefore, sat down to his task with a mind full of matter. He had at first intended to give only a paragraph to every minor poet, and only four or five pages to the greatest name. But the flood of anecdote and criticism overflowed the narrow channel. The work, which was originally meant to consist only of a few sheets, swelled into ten volumes,—small volumes, it is true, and not closely printed. The first four appeared in 1779, the remaining six in 1781.

The " Lives of the Poets " are, on the whole, the best of John-son's works. The narratives are as entertaining as any novel. The remarks on life and on human nature are eminently shrewd and profound. The criticisms are often excellent, and, even when grossly and provokingly unjust, well deserve to be studied ; for, however erroneous they may be, they are never silly. They are the judgments of a mind trammeled by prejudice, and deficient in sensibility, but vigorous and acute. They, therefore, generally contain a portion of valuable truth which deserves to be separated from the alloy ; and at the very worst they mean something,—a praise to which much of what is called criticism in our time has no pretensions.

Savage's " Life " Johnson reprinted nearly as it had appeared in 1744. Whoever, after reading that life, will turn to the other lives, will be struck by the difference of style. Since Johnson had been at ease in his circumstances, he had written little and had talked much. When, therefore, he, after the lapse of years, resumed his pen, the mannerism which he had contracted while he was in the constant habit of elaborate composition was less perceptible than formerly ; and his diction frequently had a colloquial ease which it had formerly wanted. The improvement may be discerned by a skillful critic in the " Journey to the Hebrides ;" and in the " Lives of the Poets " is so obvious, that it cannot escape the notice of the most careless reader.

Among the lives the best are, perhaps, those of Cowley,[1]

---

[1] Abraham Cowley (1618-67), essayist and poet of the so-called " metaphysical school," deemed in his day a better poet than Milton.

Dryden,[1] and Pope. The very worst is, beyond all doubt, that of Gray.[2]

This great work at once became popular. There was, indeed, much just and much unjust censure; but even those who were loudest in blame were attracted by the book in spite of themselves. Malone[3] computed the gains of the publishers at five or six thousand pounds. But the writer was very poorly remunerated. Intending at first to write very short prefaces, he had stipulated for only two hundred guineas. The booksellers, when they saw how far his performance had surpassed his promise, added only another hundred. Indeed, Johnson, though he did not despise, or affect to despise, money, and though his strong sense and long experience ought to have qualified him to protect his own interests, seems to have been singularly unskillful and unlucky in his literary bargains. He was generally reputed the first English writer of his time; yet several writers of his time sold their copyrights for sums such as he never ventured to ask. To give a single instance, Robertson[4] received four thousand five hundred pounds for the " History of Charles V. ;"[5] and it is no disrespect to the memory of Robertson to say that the " History of Charles V." is both a less valuable and a less amusing book than the " Lives of the Poets."

Johnson was now in his seventy-second year. The infirmities of age were coming fast upon him. That inevitable event of which he never thought without horror was brought near to him; and his whole life was darkened by the shadow of death. He had often to pay the cruel price of longevity. Every year he lost what could never be replaced. The strange dependents to

[1] John Dryden (1631–1700), poet and satirist; author of Absalom and Achitophel and of Hind and Panther.

[2] Thomas Gray (1716–71), author of the poems the Bard and the Elegy; one of the most learned men of his time.

[3] Edmund Malone (1741–1812), scholar and Shakespearean critic. He edited several editions of Boswell's Johnson.

[4] Dr. William Robertson (1721–93), a Scottish historian.

[5] Emperor Charles V. (1500–58) of the Holy Roman Empire.

whom he had given shelter, and to whom, in spite of their faults, he was strongly attached by habit, dropped off one by one; and in the silence of his home he regretted even the noise of their scolding matches. The kind and generous Thrale was no more; and it would have been well if his wife had been laid beside him. But she survived to be the laughingstock of those who had envied her, and to draw, from the eyes of the old man who had loved her beyond anything in the world, tears far more bitter than he would have shed over her grave. With some estimable and many agreeable qualities, she was not made to be independent. The control of a mind more steadfast than her own was necessary to her respectability. While she was restrained by her husband,—a man of sense and firmness, indulgent to her taste in trifles, but always the undisputed master of his house, —her worst offenses had been impertinent jokes, white lies, and short fits of pettishness ending in sunny good humor. But he was gone; and she was left an opulent widow of forty, with strong sensibility, volatile fancy, and slender judgment. She soon fell in love with a music master [1] from Brescia,[2] in whom nobody but herself could discover anything to admire. Her pride, and perhaps some better feelings, struggled hard against this degrading passion; but the struggle irritated her nerves, soured her temper, and at length endangered her health. Conscious that her choice was one which Johnson could not approve, she became desirous to escape from his inspection. Her manner towards him changed. She was sometimes cold, and sometimes petulant. She did not conceal her joy when he left Streatham; she never pressed him to return; and if he came unbidden she received him in a manner which convinced him that he was no longer a welcome guest. He took the very intelligible hints which she gave. He read, for the last time, a chapter of the Greek Testament in the library which had been formed by himself. In a solemn and tender prayer, he commended the house

[1] Piozzi (see note, p. 57).
[2] Capital of province of Brescia, Italy, at the foot of the Alps.

and its inmates to the Divine protection, and with emotions which choked his voice, and convulsed his powerful frame, left forever that beloved home for the gloomy and desolate house behind Fleet Street, where the few and evil days which still remained to him were to run out. Here, in June, 1783, he had a paralytic stroke, from which, however, he recovered, and which does not appear to have at all impaired his intellectual faculties. But other maladies came thick upon him. His asthma tormented him day and night. Dropsical symptoms made their appearance. While sinking under a complication of diseases, he heard that the woman whose friendship had been the chief happiness of sixteen years of his life had married an Italian fiddler,[1] that all London was crying shame upon her, and that the newspapers and magazines were filled with allusions to the Ephesian matron[2] and the two pictures in "Hamlet."[3] He vehemently said that he would try to forget her existence. He never uttered her name. Every memorial of her which met his eye he flung into the fire. She, meanwhile, fled from the laughter and hisses of her countrymen and countrywomen to a land where she was unknown, hastened across Mount Cenis,[4] and learned, while passing a merry Christmas of concerts and lemonade parties at Milan, that the great man with whose name hers is inseparably associated had ceased to exist.

He had, in spite of much mental and much bodily affliction, clung vehemently to life. The feeling described in that fine but gloomy paper which closes the series of his "Idlers" seemed to

---

[1] For a more tolerant opinion of Mrs. Thrale's conduct, see Leslie Stephens's Life of Johnson: "She lived happily with Piozzi, and never had cause to regret her marriage."

[2] A character in a Latin novel by Petronius (Arbiter), who died about A.D. 66.

[3] The pictures of his father and his uncle that Hamlet shows the Queen—

"Look here, upon this picture, and on this;
The counterfeit presentment of two brothers."—Act iii. sc. 4.

[4] A mountain pass in the Alps, 6,775 feet above the level of the sea.

grow stronger in him as his last hour drew near. He fancied that he should be able to draw his breath more easily in a southern climate, and would probably have set out for Rome and Naples, but for his fear of the expense of the journey. That expense, indeed, he had the means of defraying; for he had laid up about two thousand pounds, the fruit of labors which had made the fortune of several publishers. But he was unwilling to break in upon this hoard, and he seems to have wished even to keep its existence a secret. Some of his friends hoped that the government might be induced to increase his pension to six hundred pounds a year; but this hope was disappointed, and he resolved to stand one English winter more. That winter was his last. His legs grew weaker; his breath grew shorter; the fatal water gathered fast, in spite of incisions which he—courageous against pain, but timid against death—urged his surgeons to make deeper and deeper. Though the tender care which had mitigated his sufferings during months of sickness at Streatham was withdrawn, he was not left desolate. The ablest physicians and surgeons attended him, and refused to accept fees from him. Burke parted from him with deep emotion. Windham [1] sat much in the sick room, arranged the pillows, and sent his own servant to watch at night by the bed. Frances Burney,[2] whom the old man had cherished with fatherly kindness, stood weeping at the door; while Langton, whose piety eminently qualified him to be an adviser and comforter at such a time, received the last pressure of his friend's hand within. When at length the moment, dreaded through so many years, came close, the dark cloud passed away from Johnson's mind. His temper became unusually patient and gentle; he ceased to think with terror of death and of that which lies beyond death; and he spoke much of the mercy of God and of the propitiation of Christ. In this serene frame of mind he died on the 13th of December, 1784. He was laid, a week

---

[1] William Windham (1750–1810), politician and parliamentary orator.

[2] Frances Burney (Madame D'Arblay) (1752–1840), author of Evelina and Cecilia (see Macaulay's Madame D'Arblay).

later, in Westminster Abbey,[1] among the eminent men of whom he had been the historian,—Cowley and Denham,[2] Dryden and Congreve,[3] Gay, Prior,[4] and Addison.

Since his death, the popularity of his works—the " Lives of the Poets," and, perhaps, the " Vanity of Human Wishes," excepted —has greatly diminished. His Dictionary has been altered by editors till it can scarcely be called his. An allusion to his " Rambler" or his " Idler " is not readily apprehended in literary circles. The fame even of " Rasselas " has grown somewhat dim. But, though the celebrity of the writings may have declined, the celebrity of the writer, strange to say, is as great as ever. Boswell's book has done for him more than the best of his own books could do. The memory of other authors is kept alive by their works; but the memory of Johnson keeps many of his works alive. The old philosopher is still among us in the brown coat with the metal buttons, and the shirt which ought to be at wash, blinking, puffing, rolling his head, drumming with his fingers, tearing his meat like a tiger, and swallowing his tea in oceans. No human being who has been more than seventy years in the grave is so well known to us. And it is but just to say, that our intimate acquaintance with what he would himself have called the anfractuosities of his intellect and of his temper serves only to strengthen our conviction that he was both a great and a good man.

[1] Westminster Abbey (Westminster, London) is famous as the chief burial place of England's distinguished men. Poets' Corner records many of the most famous names in English literature.

[2] Sir John Denham (1615–68), author of Cooper's Hill.

[3] William Congreve (1670–1729), eminent dramatist; author of Double Dealer, Old Bachelor, and Mourning Bride.

[4] Matthew Prior (1664–1721), wit, poet, and diplomatist. With Montague he wrote the City and Country Mouse, a parody on Dryden's Hind and Panther. See Thackeray's English Humorists (Swift, Addison, Steele, Congreve, Prior, Pope, and others).

Fisher's Brief History of the Nations

AND OF THEIR PROGRESS IN CIVILIZATION

By GEORGE PARK FISHER, LL.D.

Professor in Yale University

Cloth, 12mo, 613 pages, with numerous Illustrations, Maps, Tables, and Reproductions of Bas-reliefs, Portraits, and Paintings. Price, $1.50

This is an entirely new work written expressly to meet the demand for a compact and acceptable text-book on General History for high schools, academies, and private schools. Some of the distinctive qualities which will commend this book to teachers and students are as follows:

It narrates in fresh, vigorous, and attractive style the most important facts of history in their due order and connection.

It explains the nature of historical evidence, and records only well established judgments respecting persons and events.

It delineates the progress of peoples and nations in civilization as well as the rise and succession of dynasties.

It connects, in a single chain of narration, events related to each other in the contemporary history of different nations and countries.

It gives special prominence to the history of the Mediaeval and Modern Periods, — the eras of greatest import to modern students.

It is written from the standpoint of the present, and incorporates the latest discoveries of historical explorers and writers.

It is illustrated by numerous colored maps, genealogical tables, and artistic reproductions of architecture, sculpture, painting, and portraits of celebrated men, representing every period of the world's history.

Copies of Fisher's Brief History of the Nations will be sent prepaid to any address, on receipt of the price, by the Publishers :

American Book Company

New York • Cincinnati • Chicago

(43)

Handbook of Greek and Roman History

GEORGES CASTEGNIER, B.S., B.L.

Flexible Cloth, 12mo, 110 pages. - Price, 50 cents

The purpose of this little handbook is to assist the student of Greek and Roman History in reviewing subjects already studied in the regular text-books and in preparing for examinations. It will also be found useful for general readers who wish to refresh their minds in regard to the leading persons and salient facts of ancient history.

It is in two parts, one devoted to Greek, and the other to Roman history. The names and titles have been selected with rare skill, and represent the whole range of classical history. They are arranged alphabetically, and are printed in full-face type, making them easy to find. The treatment of each is concise and gives just the information in regard to the important persons, places, and events of classical history which every scholar ought to know and remember, or have at ready command.

Its convenient form and systematic arrangement especially adapt it for use as an accessory and reference manual for students, or as a brief classical cyclopedia for general readers.